THE FLOWER PLANTATION

Nora Anne Brown

ALMA BOOKS

For Louisa and Peter

Prologue

I was born in a flower field thirty-three years ago. For months before my birth elephants had been roaming into my mother's fields, eating and trampling her white and yellow chrysanthemums. She had a hut built in a clearing for the nightwatchmen, whom she gave torches, whistles and drums, but the elephants went on raiding. On the night of my birth she became suspicious that the watchmen were doing nothing and set out to defend the flowers herself.

Mother told me how she struggled through endless fields, up to her bump in flowers. "The moon was full," she said, and sparks from her torch "danced around her hair". Exhausted, she arrived at the hut to find it abandoned, with bottles of beer scattered round a burnt-out fire. Furious, she bent down, picked up a bottle and hurled it into the night. As she threw that bottle, an ache shot through her belly that stole her breath and made her scream. She crouched in the clearing, frightened and alone, and as her contractions came so too did the first elephant, out of the forest, hungry and strong.

The elephant's ears flapped wildly, and its "God-awful trumpeting" filled the night air. As the pains came over her, more elephants emerged, out of the forest, one by one. The ground shuddered beneath her as they trampled the flowers, which grew only yards from where she squatted in the shadows of the dark Virunga Mountains.

"You were a surprise," she'd tell me at bedtimes as the image of trampling elephants thundered through my mind.

Mother didn't like surprises.

She said the pain and fright of giving birth in the dead of night with only the moon and marauding beasts for company made her scream so loudly that the animals took off, more terrified of her than she was of them.

"If it weren't for you, the plantation would almost certainly have been destroyed," she'd say, before adding: "You saved me from ruin before you were a minute old."

Mother would kiss my forehead, tuck the covers under my chin and say: "Never go into the forest, Arthur. Nobody knows if the elephants are still there, how hungry they are or when they might return." She'd then turn out the light and close the door behind her, whether I was asleep or not.

When I was a boy, that story kept me awake for more nights than I can remember. I was terrified that the hungry elephants might stampede again, charge into the house and kill me – or, worse, my parents – while I was sleeping. I was not a brave little boy, not what Mother must have hoped for when she named me Arthur, which some people say means courage. Perhaps courage was something she felt we both needed that night, or perhaps Mother sensed just how much of it we'd need in the years to come, when the worst thing in the world would happen in Rwanda.

But between my birth and the worst thing in the world my childhood took place – a childhood imprinted with doodles, marks and stains in a book given to me by my father when I was five years old. The book went everywhere with me until I was fourteen, when I dropped it at the border trying to save Beni, the only true friend I've ever known.

Until it arrived in the post this morning, it had been twenty years since I last held the book – my favourite childhood possession. I knew exactly what the package contained before opening it: I knew from its pocket-size shape and weight, my mother's ageing handwriting and the Rwandan postage stamp with its bright-yellow sun, turquoise sky and lime-green hills. I ran my fingers round its edges and smelt the brown wrapping paper. It was sweet and sawdusty and transported me straight back to the house where I grew up, our ivy-covered bungalow on the flower plantation.

Peeling back a corner of the paper, taking care not to tear the stamp, I revealed the navy letters of *African Butterflies* on its pale-blue cover. The book now looks tatty from almost thirty years of love followed by neglect, and part of a footprint is branded on the front cover – a dirty-brown stain impossible to remove.

Sitting in my study I opened the cover and was thrilled to rediscover the familiar orange lining paper and my name – Arthur Baptiste – in my five-year-old writing in the top corner. A letter from Mother fluttered to the ground.

Gisenyi
April 2013

Dear Arthur,

When I was packing up the bungalow I happened upon your old book. I remember quite clearly the day your father gave it to you. I am still amazed at how such a small gesture could shape an entire life.

Dr Sadler returned it to me after the soldiers took you into Zaire and back to England. In those days the book felt like part of you – I clutched it for months.

At some point I packed it away and forgot about it. I hope now it will help you to remember the Rwanda you loved, Arthur – the paradise that was your home.

Yours lovingly,
Mother.

I turned to the first page, stained with my blood – it took me straight back to being a boy in Rwanda.

PART ONE

1

RWANDA 1985

A butterfly the size of Father's hand landed on the windscreen of our stationary pickup truck. Kneeling on the driver's seat I pressed my nose against the glass and stared at the insect's belly. It was hairy. I wanted to catch it and see if it might stick to the marmalade and dirt that smeared my hands. I gazed, entranced by its body, and thought how effortlessly its paper-thin wings might tear off and of how it might taste after baking in the afternoon sun. It looked soft – and yet, I detected, it might just be crunchy too.

My thoughts of how best to trap it were cut short when Sebazungu suddenly yanked me out of the truck.

"Wake up, boy," he said, as I tried to catch my breath. "Your mother's been calling you." He bundled me over his shoulder and stole me towards the house.

As I glanced back, the glare of the midday sun bounced directly off the windscreen, and the butterfly I'd been so desperate to capture took flight on a single ray of light.

* * *

"Arthur," said Mother as Sebazungu dropped me like a sack of potatoes in the kitchen. "What have you been doing?" She handed me a blunt knife. "Go and pick a cabbage for dinner, then come in and wash your hands. And no going into the forest," she called after me as I shot out of the back door with Montague. Montague was Mother's West Highland Terrier – everyone called him Monty. We scattered the chickens in the yard.

I opened the side gate, ran towards the cabbage patch and knelt down among the neat rows. Picking cabbages was a bittersweet task: bitter because it meant eating cabbage for dinner (something I dreaded more than going to the dentist), but sweet because there was always the chance of discovering a big, juicy caterpillar that I could rescue in a jam jar and store under my bed for midnight observations.

Carefully I peeled back the grub-eaten outer leaves of a cabbage, which squeaked and snapped and smelt revolting, to reveal the shiny insides, which were smooth, cool and ripe for thwacking with my knife. On raising the blade, the butterfly I'd seen before landed beside me, its wings closed together like praying hands in church. I put down the knife, leant towards it and stared at the eye on one of its wings.

The butterfly bathed in the sun, and I forgot about chopping cabbages and thought about how to capture it instead. It was too big to cup by hand. I'd need something big, with a lid. While I was thinking about this, the butterfly opened its wings to reveal bright-blue topsides. Monty ran headlong towards it, but the butterfly flitted into the air and flew away, blending effortlessly into the afternoon light. I abandoned the cabbage patch and gave chase.

Monty and I ran down the uneven path that connected the yard to the cutting shed, past Mother's rhubarb and artichokes, Monty yapping and jumping as the butterfly bounced in flight. I followed as best I could, trying hard not to fall, keeping one eye on the ground and the other on it. The butterfly danced from one side to the other – up, down, a spurt of pace here, slower there – but all the time weaving its way through the warm, dry air.

"Eh!" cried Sebazungu as the butterfly skipped over the cut flowers that lay on the ground by the cutting shed – an open-fronted, large brick building. "*Un papillon!*" I stood with my hands on my hips beside Sebazungu, dizzy from the dance on which I'd been led, and gazed up at the insect, which rested – a brilliant blue – on the grey tile roof.

"*Il est beau,*" he said, and the gardeners stopped trimming, arranging and tying bouquets to stare at the creature.

With every bark and bounce from Monty the butterfly twitched. It seemed to look down at the huge purple agapanthus, calla lilies and sweet-smelling freesia that scattered the ground and filled countless buckets.

"*Kwirukana!* Run!" whispered Sebazungu as the butterfly looped into the air, darting over the cutting-shed roof and skipping towards the fields. I took off, Monty following closely at my ankles, over the soil that edged the fields, and jumped across the drainage ditch. I leapt so high I thought I might fly, up into the thin mountain air that barely filled my lungs. I landed with a thump in a field of golden alstroemeria.

The butterfly flew over the acres of flower fields that stretched from the cutting shed all the way to the Virunga Mountains. To the west, the volcano Nyiragongo was steaming, and to the east, on ordered terraced hills, grew cassava, potatoes and maize. To the south, in the distance, was Lake Kivu, and to the north lay the lava tunnel that led to the forest and Mount Visoke beyond.

The forest, home to the stampeding elephants of my birth, frightened me. And rumours of a red-haired witch who lived on Visoke, an inactive volcano, made it even more terrifying. Sebazungu called the witch *Kirogoya*, "wicked person", and spoke of her living with wild animals.

I imagined her living in a cage, savage and snarling and foaming at the mouth. Mother said her temper matched her red hair, and that if she wasn't careful she'd die up that mountain – which sounded like a good thing to me. When I was five years old, the forest was strictly out of bounds. I was glad of that.

It felt as if we'd run for miles by the time the butterfly stopped again. It sat on a fence post showing no sign of tiredness as Monty and I panted for breath. Monty's tongue hung down the side of his mouth, and I bent double to relieve a stitch. But before we could recover, the butterfly was off again, fluttering over a field of spotted foxgloves. We charged through the flowers, I shoulder-high in pink tubular bells and Monty rooting through the stems. Breaking out the other side of the steep field, barely able to stand, we ran straight into the clearing, which was only metres from the entrance to the tunnel and the start of the forest beyond. The butterfly skirted the edge of the trees, but I knew better than to follow any farther. To my relief, it settled on a solitary chrysanthemum by the grass hut where I was born.

I sat in the opening of the hut, my back to the forest, and watched the gardeners far below and the rain clouds rolling in over Lake Kivu. From so high up, the gardeners looked the size of flower beetles.

After a while, I realized the butterfly had disappeared – and so too had Monty. As I got up to see where they'd gone, the rain clouds broke. I took cover in the hut, certain that Monty would join me soon. The light dimmed. Thunder rumbled around the hillsides. Monty didn't come. The gardeners huddled in the cutting shed. Sebazungu ran for cover. Mother stood at the back door, no doubt calling my name. But still, no Monty. I hunkered down on the straw of the hut and watched a green gecko stalk a blue fly.

The rain stopped after an hour, and darkness closed in. Celeste, the housekeeper, lit fires. The smell of charcoal fogged the evening air. I was getting cold, but Monty was nowhere to be seen. I stood up and clapped my hands.

Nothing. I looked towards the tunnel and the forest. I knew I had no choice.

I took my first step into the dark, damp tunnel, thirty foot long and five foot wide. That's when I learnt: when you try not to think about elephants, elephants are all you can think about.

Edging my way towards the forest, attempting not to touch the cold slimy walls that looked as though they'd been formed by rough hides scratching against them, I forced myself to think only of Monty and where he might have gone. I decided on the heart of the forest: that's where I thought he'd have found shelter from the rain. But the heart of the forest would be a fine hiding place for hungry elephants, I thought. A fine place for a boy like me to be trampled to death!

After what felt like a long time, I stepped out of the tunnel and into the crowded trees. My heart banged so hard against my ribs I was certain the elephants would hear. As I crept through the twisted undergrowth of fern, moss and lichen, my breathing grew tight and shallow. Every twig that cracked beneath me made me gasp and jump. *Just think of Monty*, I said internally, over and over. *Think of Monty*. What would he do? Where would he go? I decided he'd follow the smell of rats and started to look for nests in the damp mossy ground. I saw nothing. No Monty. No nests. Nothing but elephant-shaped shadows.

On I went, deeper and deeper, picking my way through gnarly trunks until I stumbled on one of the roots. I heard something snap. Then my ankle burned. I lay on the ground in agony.

The next thing I knew I was coming round, freezing cold and hearing only the sound of a whimper. I held my breath, trying to understand what the noise was and where it was coming from. It was constant, a continuous pining – it didn't sound like an elephant, or a witch either. I sat up, clutched my ankle and listened some more. The pining was now broken by yelps.

Monty!

Hold on Monty, I wanted to shout, *I'm coming*. But even then, when I needed to speak most, I couldn't. Those were the days before I was brave enough to talk, before I knew that it was more powerful to have a voice than not. Not a single sound came out.

Grabbing hold of a tree I hauled myself up. I tried to put weight on my ankle, but the pain was too fierce. I clung to the tree and steadied myself, took a deep breath and hopped on one foot to the next. I did this again and again. Hop – hold – steady – breathe. Hop – hold – steady – breathe. In the end, I must have done it fifty times or more before I found old Monty.

He was hanging by a hind leg, whimpering and squirming. I clung to a tree, terrified at what I saw. I found the courage to hop over to him and reached up. The wire cut into his hip so deeply that blood soaked his white coat. I managed to loosen the knot, his blood covering my hands. The noose came free and we fell to the ground, exhausted.

From the forest floor the wire swung above us like a noose. I thought about the witch and the wild animals she lived with, whom she'd probably snared too – and I felt angry. I wanted to catch her and pull out her red hair and see how she liked it. I wanted to do all sorts of mean things I'd never done before.

While I was having those angry thoughts I had a sudden feeling that we were being watched. I stroked Monty for courage and rose to my feet. But as I stood, resolute in my anger, something banged – a bang that sounded long and low throughout the forest. It made my limbs freeze, my heart leap and my newfound courage disappear. And then, when the forest became still and quiet again, I heard someone running quickly, furiously away.

2

The next morning, when the cockerel crowed, I had no memory of what had happened between hearing someone running away in the forest and waking up in bed with my ankle bandaged. I wondered if Monty was safe in his bed too. I wanted to check on him, but my blue wristwatch told me it was quarter-past six, so I had to wait five minutes for Joseph, the nightwatchman, to walk down the path beside my bedroom, just as he did every morning. Nothing could break my routine when I was five, not even Monty being snared.

A few minutes later I heard Joseph pass, his large rubber boots slapping against the backs of his calves. He whistled his way through the waking garden and home to bed. I got up and limped to the back lobby, where Monty was lying on his pile of blankets licking his wound. I wondered how we'd both got home – I couldn't have walked down the hill on my bad ankle and have carried him too.

With this mystery in mind I ate two small green bananas and fed Monty the scraps from dinner, then went outside to try and ride my yellow tricycle in the yard.

My ankle felt strong in its bandage, so I rode the trike in my blue-and-white pyjamas over the bumpy, compacted dirt. I mapped the shadowy outlines of the scraggly cypress trees that dwarfed the back of the yard and cruised past the gate leading to the flower fields and the forest beyond. With an injection of pace, I cycled past the opposite gate, which opened to Mother's side garden, then swerved in and out of the two brick outhouses – one for storing wood, another for doing the washing – my trike riding smoothly on their concrete floors. I parked beside Joseph's mud-and-banana-leaf lookout and went in. The sour smell of his body hung in the air, and his sleeping bag was still warm.

In the opposite corner of the yard, Celeste was heating water for my bath on the charcoal stoves under the corrugated roof. She was blind in her left eye, so she couldn't see me. I spied on her. She leant heavily against her *fimbo* and adjusted her red headscarf. Celeste was always fidgeting with her clothes – pulling at her T-shirt or adjusting her wrap. Nothing seemed to fit her heavy, lopsided body.

When my watch read seven o'clock, I got off my trike and followed Celeste into the house. We both hobbled – her flip-flops slapped on the ground. In the back lobby I moved Monty's food away from him to see if he'd get up, but his injury was worse than mine and he stayed on his blankets, still licking his wound.

I went to the kitchen, crouched down and picked up a toy car. I rode it steadily over the linoleum towards the living room, which was also our dining room. There I rose to my knees, trying to avoid burns from the rugs, and bumped the car against the textured paint on the walls. At the entrance to the bedroom corridor I ran the car at speed down the red concrete floor. I loved the whirr of the wheels and the crash and thud as it hit the end wall.

Entering our black-and-white bathroom, I found Celeste rescuing a cockroach from the tub with her bare hands – she put it out the window. I never understood how cockroaches managed to squeeze their big hard bodies through the tiny slots in the plughole. Having spared the cockroach, she sloshed the pails of hot water into the tub and helped me undress.

"T-shirt off," she said, as she did every morning, and flashed me her gummy grin. Celeste knew to touch only my clothes, not me. I didn't like to be touched. With me undressed, she popped my clothes in the laundry basket and left me to bathe.

I got in and washed, paying attention to the dirt from the forest underneath my finger and toenails. When my wash was complete, I played a makeshift *guiro* on my ribs – my favourite thing to do in the bath – then waited for Celeste to return and wrap a towel around me. Celeste always wrapped me up, but I rubbed myself down.

"Off you go," she said when I was done, pointing towards my bedroom.

There were very few toys in my room – some Lego bricks, marbles and a couple of storybooks about wicked queens and poisoned maidens – and it wasn't at all comfortable, with its concrete floor, cast-iron bed and scratchy woollen blankets. A brick fireplace sat opposite my bed, and a small window, framed with ivy and purple hydrangeas, overlooked the front garden, which was full of Mother's favourite yellow roses and buddleia bushes.

Every morning when I was bathing, Celeste laid out my clothes in my bedroom. That day was "blue shorts and red T-shirt" day, the same clothes I wore every Monday. But on my return from the bathroom I didn't find my blue shorts and red T-shirt: instead I found a set of khaki shorts and T-shirt with matching socks on the bed. I could smell polish from the new brown leather shoes that Celeste had lined up precisely on the floor. Something was wrong.

I walked down the corridor, past Father's room, to Mother's, went to her bed and folded back the bedclothes.

"What is it, Arthur?" she said, still half-asleep. She rubbed her eyes, the colour of green marbles, and sat up, attempting to flatten her long hair. I took her hand and led her to my room. Mother didn't grumble: she knew something was wrong too.

In the bedroom I pointed at the clothes, suggesting that Celeste had made a mistake, and please could Mother fix it. But instead of resolving the problem, Mother crouched down in front of me and clutched my upper arms. It hurt.

"Arthur, it's time," she said.

Time for what, I puzzled, as Mother took off my towel and dried my hair roughly. That hurt even more. "It's time for you to start school, Arthur, with all the other boys and girls."

As she tugged the T-shirt over my head and manhandled me into the shorts – which made me want to burst – all I could think about was: *Which boys and girls?*

I didn't know any boys and girls. I only knew Mother and Father. And Sebazungu and Joseph, Celeste and Fabrice the cook. And what would I do at school? Chop heads off chickens? Eat cabbage?

I sat on the corner of my bed and thought about this while Mother got dressed.

At twenty past eight Mother led me away from my bed. She took me by the hand and walked me down the five steps of our bungalow, my stiff khaki shorts rubbing against my thighs. We went down the grass path to the hydrangea bushes at the bottom of the garden, where giant purple and pink blooms separated Mother's formal English garden from the orange road and the bright-red anthuriums that grew wild in Rwanda. We turned out of the garden gate and headed towards the three mud shops clustered at the side of the road.

Mother said "*Muraho*" to the ladies, who chuckled and stopped stacking their yellow bread and brown avocados.

"*Bonjour*," they replied.

Those women loved to laugh when Mother and I passed by. The whites of their eyes were yellow, matching the fabric they wore and the bread that they sold. I looked back at the footprints my new shoes had made in the orange dirt. Even the make of the shoe, embossed in the sole, was visible. A fine set of tracks, I thought.

"What have I told you about going into the forest?" Mother said once we were past the laughing ladies. Mother always asked me questions, even though she knew I wouldn't talk. I hadn't spoken since I was three, when I used to speak to Monty and my bug collection – but even that felt uncomfortable. One day, when I thought I was alone and was whispering to Monty, I discovered Mother listening at the door. It felt as if someone had sneaked up on me and shouted very loudly, making my heart race. Since that day I never spoke again – not once. The mere idea made me feel my throat would close up and I'd stop breathing.

"It's not for playing in, Arthur. It's not safe for little boys." I knew it wasn't safe – the snares were deadly. Sometimes Mother had to shoot trapped animals that were too badly injured to survive.

"Hopefully last night taught you that." She looked at me as if she was both cross and sad. "If it wasn't for Sebazungu finding you, who knows what might have happened." She paused to clear a tickle in her throat.

I thought about the elephants, and the red-haired witch, and Sebazungu, who should have been at home with his wife and young son. What was he doing in the forest? I wanted to ask, but couldn't.

"It could have been you in that snare, Arthur, not Monty. People get caught in wires or are strangled to death in antelope nooses – or even fall into pit traps. It could have been much worse than just a sprained ankle. Do you understand?" I nodded. Mother was right, but I thought she'd be thankful I'd rescued Monty. She wasn't.

Past the shops and a little way round the bend was a low building made of brown bricks. There were lots of noisy, barefoot children running outside. It was the school. I hid behind Mother's skirt. I'd have preferred to be in the forest with elephants than in school among all those children.

"Be good, Arthur," said Mother, after she'd weaved me through the compound and into a dingy room that smelt like our hen coop. As Mother spoke to the teacher, I sat on a low wooden bench with a higher one in front of it that served as a desk. I swung my legs and looked at my new shoes and wriggled about to avoid wooden splinters prickling my thighs. I watched a fluttering butterfly at the window as it tried to escape and thought about how I might do the same. Then I looked at the picture of President Habyarimana hanging at an angle on the peeling wall, and at the dirt floor and the huge blackboard with no chalk. A map of Rwanda was taped to the wall, and looked as if it could fall at any moment.

"I'll pick you up at lunchtime," said Mother, kissing my forehead and leaving me alone with the teacher. His skin was as rough as the potholed road to town, and his eyes sagged so badly you could see the pink tissue beneath them.

He rang a handbell. The children rushed in and pushed past, which made me want to scream. They sat bunched together like the swallows on the clothesline in our yard. I pretended not to notice their curious looks or muffled giggles. The teacher, in his black shirt, made them recite *être* and *avoir*, and the "three times" table. I did it all in my head, it was easy.

Midway through the morning I became aware of someone looking at me from behind. I didn't like that. I stared into the distance and began to groan quietly. Time slowed, sounds faded, soon I was in a world of my own, far away from the schoolroom, teacher and children. I was lost in one of my "absences" – something that happened a lot when I was little – and remained so until Mother came back at lunch.

She said to the teacher, "If he comes often enough, he'll get used to it. He may even begin to talk."

But the teacher disagreed: he scrunched up his brow and shook his head, saying, "He can't come back. He's disturbing the other children."

Mother sighed, took my hand and led me away.

"Typical," she muttered, marching me out of the compound, round the bend and past the shops, her blond hair flaring out behind her. She didn't say "*Muraho*" to the ladies, but they laughed all the same, their yellow eyes following us up the road. Mother pressed onwards, retracing our steps towards home.

As Mother grumbled about the teacher, I felt my new shoes cut into the backs of my heels. I could feel blood seeping into the leather, but I knew better than to groan any more. Too much groaning frustrated Mother and caused her to go to her room, close the door and only come out when Father came home. I didn't like it when Mother did that, so I kept quiet, despite the pain.

"Your Father will be back this evening," said Mother, closing the gate. I felt safe again in the quiet of the garden, and knowing Father would be home in time for dinner cheered me up. Being with Father would make me forget the pain of school and my new shoes.

* * *

"We'll have to devise a plan," said Mother over supper.

I picked at the goat stew Fabrice had made. He'd served it with pasta, which made Mother angry.

"When will he learn?" she asked. "Rice or potatoes are fine, but pasta?" She let out an enormous sigh. I thought it was terrible of Mother to complain about Fabrice's food: Mother couldn't even cook beans. She placed her elbow on the plastic tablecloth and leant her cheek on her fist. "Well?" she said, raising her eyebrows at Father.

"Well what?" he asked, looking up with his big brown eyes with lashes as long as a giraffe's. My toes skimmed the antelope skin under the table as I looked out at the dusk creeping over Mother's side garden. She didn't answer. "I'll have a word with him."

"Not about the pasta," she said. "About school!"

The mention of school made me drop my fork in the stew. I fished it out.

"Arthur, for goodness' sake!" sighed Mother.

"Don't worry, Arthur," said Father, handing me a clean fork. "We'll sort things out."

He placed his hand gently on my shoulder. We ate our goat stew and pasta in silence.

* * *

Later that evening Mother and Father quarrelled in the lounge. I pressed my ear to the living-room door and heard Mother say: "He should go to boarding school in England."

"I was sent to England when I was five years old," said Father, "and no son of mine will be subjected to the same thing."

"But he'll be ostracized here. He's not like other children."

I didn't know what "ostracized" meant, but I knew I wasn't like the other children: I was a different colour.

"You should teach him yourself," said Father.

"As if I've nothing else to do." Mother's voice sounded closer. The door opened and I lost my balance, toppling onto her shoes. "Arthur, go to bed!"

I went to my room and thumbed the worn pages of the family photograph album, while Mother and Father continued to squabble in the lounge.

"Maybe if you spoke to Dr Sadler again, things would be easier for you," said Father. Dr Sadler was the doctor who gave monthly pills to Mother and pink medicine to me when I was sick. Mother saw Dr Sadler a lot.

"There's nothing wrong with me, Albert. It's him."

Mother must have thought I was asleep. I wasn't. I sat on my window seat, wide awake, my cheek pushed against the glass. Moonlight stole in and fell over the faded pictures, illuminating silent, dead family members.

"And Dr Sadler doesn't know what's wrong with him anyway," continued Mother. "He doesn't know what causes his absences. And he has no clue why Arthur's so afraid to talk: all he can come up with is something to do with anxiety, some sort of phobia." I thought about the elephants. "There's nothing wrong with him physically, Albert. Maybe in England someone could help. A psychiatrist."

"Let's not get ahead of ourselves, Martha. He's still young."

"But he's not safe here. What was he doing in the forest, for Christ's sake? Anything could have happened. If it wasn't for…" Mother didn't finish. I heard the chink of the decanter on her glass.

"Let's just be thankful he got home safely," said Father, and he went out to the front veranda for a cigarette.

I heard the shuffle of Mother's slippers on the red concrete floor coming towards my room. The door opened a little, creating a shaft of light.

"It's time for you to go to bed," she said, shutting the album. She scooped me up, laid me down and told me the story of my birth. When she was finished and the thought of elephants rampaging through the house was well and truly embedded in my mind, she kissed me on the forehead and left, closing the door tightly shut. Then I heard her close her door too. Father was still on the veranda.

The arguments about my schooling went on for weeks. Mostly they ended with Mother going to her room, Father smoking a cigarette and me sitting alone in the dark.

In the end it was Father who won.

3

1986

Some time after my sixth birthday, Mother began to teach me at home. She refused to "act as schoolmarm" and told me, "You're not going to spend the next twelve years with your nose in a textbook." A timetable was devised, more by trial and error than by design.

On Mondays I'd help the gardeners in the fields. Depending on what time of year it was, I'd learn to plant seeds, thin saplings, weed, deadhead and harvest. I got to know how to treat insect infestations and how crops differed from dry season to wet. Mother always used to tell me that being taught about life on the plantation was "far more useful than anything you'll find in a book".

Tuesday was the day we went to town. Mother called this "life skills", which mostly meant shopping – something she was particularly good at and something I particularly loathed.

On Wednesday mornings, Mother made me study art, which I liked about as much as shopping, but Wednesday afternoons were great. That was when Father stopped wearing his tie and serious expression and replaced them with a short-sleeve shirt and smile. He'd come home from the city at lunchtime, put his briefcase in his study and close the door saying, "Where's my boy?" What I loved best about those afternoons was the time we spent together in the garden and the stories Father told about Rwanda.

Thursdays I spent with Sebazungu learning Kinyarwanda and French and, from time to time, some maths. Sebazungu was the foreman. He was a solid man with dark, pock-marked skin and a scar on his jaw that looked like a new moon. He spoke English, French, Kinyarwanda and Kswahili, he knew how to drive, and Father said his brain was quicker than a calculator. The gardeners were afraid of him, but Mother adored him. Without Sebazungu the plantation wouldn't have been running at all. He knew it better than anyone, even Mother. When Mother came to Rwanda, it was Sebazungu who showed her how the plantation worked – and when I was six he did the same for me.

"You'll learn more from him than from me," Mother would tell me whenever I was dragging my feet. "Before you know it, you'll be doing long divisions in your sleep, speaking four languages and managing the plantation yourself." I didn't see how. Sebazungu spoke so quickly and switched between languages so often that I was lucky to understand my own name, let alone anything else.

Fridays were for English, and one Saturday a month everyone had to do voluntary work, because of a government directive. I was made to do the chores Fabrice and Celeste would usually do, such as washing floors and peeling potatoes. Saturdays were the worst – and Sundays weren't much better.

Sunday mornings were spent in church, since religious education was not Mother's forte. "I'll leave it to the priest," she used to say, even though the priest preached in Kinyarwanda and I barely understood him. And then in the afternoon the gardeners and their families would come for music and dance in the side garden, so that I might learn "a little bit of culture".

That was how my weekly routine went and, on the whole, it suited me just fine.

* * *

"Life is an education!" Mother told me for what felt like the hundredth time that year, as we thundered down the potholed track on our way to Gisenyi.

The flowers bounced around in buckets in the back of our pickup – pink and red blooms blazing through the orange-and-green countryside. Sebazungu squatted in the back, guarding every stem. Monty sat on my lap, his paws resting on the open window. Since the incident in the forest he'd lost one of his hind legs, making him much less fun

– but I loved him all the same. At that time he was my only friend. Mother told me he'd come with her from England. She said when Father was working in the city she'd talk to Monty, because "no one else for miles around understood English". It never occurred to me when I was six that Monty couldn't understand it either.

The condition of the eight-kilometre track from home to the main road was terrible, and it took most people thirty minutes by car. It took Mother ten. I never knew if Mother was the best or worst of drivers: all I knew was that I loved the bone-shaking ride. When we hit the narrowest section of road with the largest potholes and the sharpest bends Mother would yell, "Hold on tight, boy, here comes the fun!"

I loved looking back in the side mirror at the orange dust the truck kicked up. It blurred the brown faces of women with enormous bundles of wood on their heads and babies on their backs. I loved watching the men at the side of the road who filled in the potholes and stood with their hands stretched out, waiting for passing drivers to give them spare change. I loved the noise of the gears crunching and the exhaust pipe scraping on the boulders. I loved the warm scent of smoke and manure that filtered through the dashboard vents, and I loved the way I had to peel my legs off the hot sticky seat.

The pleasure came to an end when we turned onto the smooth tarmac that led steeply down to town. The road to Gisenyi terrified me almost as much as the forest. Huge lorries swayed from one side of the road to the other; *boda-bodas* laden with entire families – including their goats and chickens – dodged in and out of the traffic, while *matatus* bursting with passengers stopped, without warning, every few hundred yards. Most vehicles had their indicators on, yet few ever turned.

Mother's hand hovered over the horn as endless people, in no hurry to get anywhere, dawdled by the roadside. Every now and then she'd push down with the heel of her hand and swerve to miss a sauntering cow or a small child dressed in an oversized T-shirt bunched in the middle with a piece of rope. The horn was completely hopeless: even the one on my trike was louder. The people we passed watched as we charged on, down into the heat that we managed to avoid up in the mountains. The further we went – past the Honda C90s loaded with household furniture balanced precariously, past the lorries whose brakes had failed, now cast aside like tin cans by the side of the road, and past the prisoners in their orange uniforms ploughing the fields – the hotter it got.

At last we rounded the bend and descended into Gisenyi, on the shores of Lake Kivu. That's where Mother slowed down. The town moved slowly past the window of our pickup, like film through Father's home projector. We drove past the lake, sparkling and blue, in the direction of the border with Zaire. We passed the schoolchildren in their khaki shorts, the foam-mattress shops and the decaying colonial buildings in every colour of ice cream.

Our first stop was the petrol station. Sebazungu leapt from the back of the pickup to supervise the pump attendant. While the fuel was being put in, the attendant's son, an old-looking boy with a heavy brow in a black leatherette jacket and long trousers, appeared from the giant tree in the far corner of the forecourt. He'd been harvesting mangoes. Changing his machete for his bucket and rag, he strode towards us, leapt onto the bonnet and set about cleaning the windscreen.

Our eyes met as he lathered the glass. Trying to avoid his stare, I looked towards the volcano and its billow of steam – the only cloud in the sky.

"*Oya, oya*," said Mother. "No, no! Little pest." She dismissed him with a swat of her hand. "Anything for a few francs," she muttered, and he ran off. We watched the boy climb the mango tree, machete between his teeth, his eyes firmly on me.

The attendant's fat wife approached our pickup with cold sodas.

"*Mwaramutse*," said Mother.

"*Bonjour*," replied the woman.

Mother pointed at a brown and an orange soda and gave the woman two coins. The woman removed the caps from the bottles and handed them to us. I tried not to look at

the boy in the tree and drank my soda to the warbling call
of a cuckoo bird.

With the truck refuelled, Sebazungu gave our soda bottles back to the attendant's wife and then jumped into the
back. Mother turned on the ignition and we set off again,
continuing our journey round the lake.

After a short while we drove past Madame Dubois's
house. Mother said she'd lived in Gisenyi "since the dawn
of time". Whenever we passed her house, she'd be outside
in a long dress and floppy hat, clipping her topiary hedge,
which formed the words: "I Love Jesus".

A little farther down the road, past the stall that sold rag
dolls to tourists, was the post office. It was a big pastel-pink
building set back from the main road. Its narrow entrance
was on top of an open storm drain, which Mother hated
driving over. Every time we went to the post office I'd hang
out of the window and watch as the tyres inched perilously
close to slipping six feet into the gutter. We never did fall,
but there was always the danger that we might, and that
was fun enough.

Mother and I left Sebazungu and Monty in the pickup
at the side of the building and walked around to the shady
front entrance. I ran my hand along the peeling paintwork
and stopped to pick at pieces that came away like bark from
eucalyptus trees.

"Arthur," Mother called, and I caught up with her, a
handful of dry paint crumbling between my fingers.

The postmaster looked up as we entered. He was an elderly man who worked alone in the cavernous building, which was more like a railway station with its wooden benches, large broken clock and glass partitions. It smelt of sawdust and glue.

The old man squinted from behind the glass as Mother approached, peering around the little clouds that floated in the centre of his eyes. Mother told me he had cataracts and that I "wasn't to stare". When she was within a few feet of him and clearly visible, he said:

"Eh, Madame Baptiste. *Comment ça va?*"

"*Ne meza*," Mother answered. "Has my parcel arrived?" Mother had been waiting for shoes from England for weeks. This was her third attempt to collect them.

"*Non, Madame, je suis désolé, mais—*"

From under the counter the old man produced a parcel wrapped in brown paper and placed it in front of her. It was covered in stamps of the Queen of England.

"*Pour le Docteur.*"

Mother sighed, I didn't know why: I thought the parcel was exciting.

The postmaster opened the huge ledger and went to look for a pen. Mother and I took a seat on a bench by the window, where I stared at the picture of the President. It was as if he was watching me. I admired the post office: everything about it was great. There was a parquet floor made up of thousands of interlocking pieces and hundreds of little wooden boxes, each with its own tiny door, number and miniature key. There were narrow shelves that sat in perfect order with nothing on them. And everything had to be completed in triplicate. Being the postmaster seemed like the perfect job.

"How can something that looks so efficient actually be utter chaos?" Mother asked, staring at the ceiling while drumming her nails on the bench.

The shadows in the room had shifted by the time the old man returned with his pen. Mother printed her name and address and signed three times on three separate pages of the very large book. She handed me the parcel, which I held like a prized possession. Mother thanked the old man, who winked at me, as though he thought the parcel was exciting too. Then we stepped back into the searing heat. I climbed into the pickup and placed the stamp-covered parcel on the centre seat.

We took the short cut to market. The steep dirt road made the engine roar. Mother moved from third gear to second, and we leant forward, as if to stop the pickup from slipping back down towards the lake. I loved doing that with Mother: it was our private little game. At the top of the hill she parked in the shade of an acacia tree, instructed Sebazungu to buy a sack of rice, took my hand and led me into the marketplace with Monty limping behind us.

"It won't take long," she told me above the noise of haggling market vendors, blaring radios and bleating goats.

We wove in and out of piles of mismatched shoes heaped up on the dirt and past stalls selling ladies' underwear. "I just need some fabric."

I knew that would take for ever. Fabric-shopping was torture.

Big-bosomed women began to bustle around Mother as if *she* were the Queen of England. Each of them rushed off and reappeared with piles of cloth with patterns so intricate they made my head spin.

I sat down on a little stool, sank into myself and thought about Father's parcel. I wondered what was in it.

Gradually the sounds and smells of the marketplace shrank into one, and there I remained, with three-legged Monty by my side, until Mother was done.

* * *

"One last stop, Arthur, and then we can go for tea with Dr Sadler," said Mother, a roll of purple-and-green batik wedged under her arm. We wound our way out of the busy market, past potato sacks as tall as me, towering pyramids of tomatoes and endless boxes of dried fish, the smell of which made me feel sick.

At the exit of the market, where *boda-boda* drivers usually huddled round Mother offering to carry her shopping and drive us home, a crowd had formed. People were saying "*Kirogoya, Kirogoya*" in hushed voices. I couldn't remember what that word meant until Mother and I got closer and I spotted a tall white woman with a mass of red hair in the centre of the crowd. Sebazungu whispered in my ear, "Wicked Person."

The witch! I tugged at Mother's hand.

"Just a minute, Arthur," she said, stopping at the edge of the crowd to see what was going on. Clearly Mother didn't know what she was looking at or the danger we were in. Monty let out a high-pitched bark and ran off in the direction of the pickup.

Mother watched the witch: I hid behind her, too terrified to look. Had people gathered to see her snarling and foaming at the mouth like the wild animals she'd snared and caged in the forest? Could she attack at any moment? I didn't want to find out. I pressed my face into the top of Mother's legs and groaned.

"It's OK, Arthur," said Mother, and I peaked round her leg. The witch raised her hand in the air, making her as tall as a giant pine tree, and waved in our direction. I ducked back behind Mother.

"Martha," she called. I wondered how the witch knew Mother's name and decided she must have magic powers. "Martha," she called again, but Mother didn't respond: she moved away in a hurry, the way I did when I was listening at doors and heard someone coming.

"Let's go, Arthur," she said, whisking me along and ignoring the witch's calls. We crossed the road without stopping to check both ways for cars and went into the shop that was only frequented by Americans and Europeans.

"Bertie!" said Mother, entering the store. Mother's friend, Mrs Blanchett, whom everyone referred to as Madame B., was buying chocolate. She was a plump French lady who owned the local tea plantation. Whenever she saw me she'd try to squeeze my cheeks and pinch my nose: that day was no exception. Before she could get her hands on me I slunk away to the fridge and took in the cold air and the pong of the French cheese and Italian ham, trying to think about Father's parcel and not about the witch.

"How *are* you, Martha?" asked Madame B. I didn't catch Mother's reply. "And Arthur?" This time Mother didn't answer. Instead she asked about Madame B.'s husband. Then they talked about shoes and someone called Laura Laney.

"It's so rare for her to be in town during the day," said Madame B., and Mother agreed with a disdainful laugh.

"Come for coffee soon," said Mother, and she kissed the air by Madame B.'s face.

Mother paid for her shampoo and handed me a lollipop. We went back to the pickup, where the crowd had dispersed and the witch was gone.

* * *

"Remember not to touch things," warned Mother as she fixed her hair and put on lipstick in the car park of the Kivu Hotel, just a stone's throw from the border. I repositioned Father's parcel in the centre seat. "Keep your hands to yourself and don't stare." Mother said this each time we arrived at the Kivu – I didn't know why. I neither touched anything nor paid any attention to the hotel guests who came to see the gorillas.

Father had told me about the gorillas on Mount Visoke, one of the few places in the world where they still lived in the wild. He told me a group of gorillas was called a band. He said there were very few left, and that some people thought the gorillas' bodies had special powers that could "turn dying men into dancing men". Those people killed the gorillas, chopping off their heads, hands and feet. I figured the witch must be one of them, and that made me angry.

Father also said the gorillas were hugely strong and protective of their babies, and that they could easily kill a man who got in the way of their young. But he said I shouldn't be afraid, because they lived too far up the mountain and would not bother with someone as little as me. From time to time I'd look up to Visoke and hope that one day I might see one, just to know what they smelt and sounded like. But most of all I hoped that one of them would kill the witch. The gardeners said she snared, caged and trained them. I hoped that one would break free and that would be the end of her.

As I thought about the gorillas and the witch, someone knocked on the driver's window. It was the beggar who sold wooden objects – masks, little motorbikes, salad tongs. He wore black shades, flip-flops and a heavy wool coat, even in the scorching heat. Every time we came to town he badgered Mother to buy something. She never bought a thing.

"Get away," shouted Mr Umuhoza, the hotel manager, who was coming over to greet us. The beggar scrammed. Sebazungu carted flowers to the cold-storage room.

Mr Umuhoza was a tall man who looked like a camel: long legs, a big belly, flabby lips and rotten teeth. I didn't like Mr Umuhoza: he always ruffled my hair like Father. This time, when he tried, I ducked out of his way.

"Good to see you, Arthur," he said. He placed his hand in the small of Mother's back and took us through to the lounge, which had leafy wallpaper and giant glass windows overlooking the pool. There was a long bar and lots of tables and wicker chairs with thick cushions. Usually it was full of men wearing safari jackets and large-bottomed women in shorts and long socks; this day was no exception.

Dr Sadler was waiting for Mother, sipping tea and, as always, blotting his brow with a red handkerchief. He was a large, friendly man with grey curly hair and soft eyes. I never saw him in anything other than a crumpled beige linen suit. I wanted to know why he didn't have someone kind like Celeste to iron his clothes. One day, I thought, I might be able to ask.

"Hello Martha," he said, standing to greet Mother and squeezing her hand.

"Edward," she said and pressed her cheek against his.

"And hello, Arthur." He smiled brightly, but didn't try to touch me. I liked Dr Sadler for that. "Do you feel like saying hello today?" I didn't.

Mother and the doctor sat down. Her legs leant against his. She looked like someone in the magazines she had sent over from England and laughed like one of the American actresses she watched on her video player. She had forgotten about me already.

I went outside and skirted the side of the pool, where ladies in brightly coloured swimming costumes lay on loungers. Monty limped behind me as I followed the little stone path that led to the beach.

Sitting down under a palm tree I watched the local children splash in the water. I hoped they wouldn't see me, the pale-skinned boy under the tree. The Mzungu Boy. My hope was in vain.

"*Mzungu!*" yelled one boy and ran up the sand. His sinewy wet muscles shone in the sun.

"*Mzungu!*" he said again, and waved his arm for the other children to join him. One by one they saw what he saw and ran up the beach. Within moments their lean black bodies enveloped me. Salt water and sand splattered my skin.

"*Mzungu! Mzungu!*" they chanted and jumped about wildly, brandishing jerrycans and sticks and kicking sand in my face. I wanted to explain that Father was half Rwandan. Only Mother was white. But the words stuck in my throat.

Monty yapped and growled and defended me as best he could, but it didn't stop them. It wasn't long before one of their sticks caught me on the head and I fell to the ground. They scurried down the beach like rats.

After a few moments I struggled to my feet and staggered back up the stone path, where I found Mr Umuhoza and Sebazungu standing by the pool.

"Arthur," said Mr Umuhoza, ruffling my hair. My head hurt too much to pull away. "What happened?"

"He won't answer," laughed Sebazungu, picking me up and looking at my head. "That's a big bump, Arthur. Let's get your mother."

Mother wasn't in the lounge, so Sebazungu put me on a couch while Mr Umuhoza went off to find her. Monty kept guard. Mother arrived a few minutes later, followed hastily by Dr Sadler. Sweat clung to her upper lip, and her lipstick was faded.

"Arthur," she said, standing over me and feeling the area around the bruise. "Are you all right? You gave me a fright."

Dr Sadler knelt to examine me. My head was pounding.

"Can you tell me how you feel, Arthur?" I couldn't. Dr Sadler's eyes told me that was OK. He smiled at me.

"No long-term damage," he concluded with a laugh and mopped his brow.

"How did this happen?" Mother asked.

"The local children, Madame," replied Sebazungu.

"Where were you? Why weren't you keeping an eye on him?" Mother didn't give Sebazungu a chance to reply.

On her command he scooped me up and carried me to the pickup. She drove recklessly back to the flower plantation. I didn't love it this time: I felt sick.

When we arrived, she slammed on the brakes, creating a cloud of dust that engulfed us. She jumped out, tore open the passenger door and shouted, "Take him inside, Sebazungu!" – which he did, placing me on my bed and leaving Mother and me alone.

Mother paced like a leopard round the bedroom and muttered something about Father being displeased. She bit her fingernails. As dark descended, the evening chorus of crickets became louder, as if someone had turned up the volume on a record player. Beneath the din of crickets I heard the horn of Father's car at the gate and the sound of Joseph, boots slapping, running down the gravel drive.

A hushed conversation followed in the kitchen, then the beat of Father's wooden soles came down the red corridor. My bedroom door opened.

Father rested his large hand on my chest and tucked loose hairs behind my ears. He placed the brown package with the stamps of the Queen of England under my fingers.

I don't know if he spoke: if he did, I didn't hear him.

He left, leaving my door open just a crack. A wedge of light from the hall crept over my bed, just enough so that I could see the parcel and open it.

Peeling back a corner of brown paper, taking care not to tear the stamps, I revealed the pale blue of a pocket book. In the half-light I could make out the navy words on the hard cover. They read "African Butterflies".

4

1987

Between the ages of six and seven I took *African Butterflies* everywhere with me. It kept me in the plantation and out of the forest. I became obsessed with caterpillar eggs and spent hours each day hunting for them in the side garden. On the day before my seventh birthday I had my biggest find of all.

"*Gishyushye!* Hot!" warned Fabrice, opening the door of the wood-burning stove in the kitchen to reveal eight sterilized jam jars sitting in rows. Clutching my slightly dog-eared book I rushed to glimpse the gleaming glass. On Fabrice's instruction I stood back and watched him remove the jars with a clean cloth – he knew they had to be spotless. Fabrice understood my obsession better than most: he had obsessions of his own, such as wearing shiny red shoes that creaked and saying things three times.

"The jars are scorching hot," said Mother, entering the kitchen and turning down Fabrice's radio. "Go and prepare for art in the garden. Fabrice will bring them to you when you've finished your lesson."

I wanted to stay with Fabrice and my jam jars, but I knew better than to disobey Mother. And anyway, now that I had *African Butterflies,* art lessons weren't such a chore. Mother allowed me to use the book as inspiration for my drawings, and I gladly pored over the anatomical diagrams of the butterfly in all its stages, trying to copy them. Mother said it combined art and biology, and that was "more than I'd ever learn in any school in Rwanda".

Having fetched my paper, pencil and crayons from the bureau in the living room I took them to the side garden. There I set the materials on the table next to Mother's white wooden bench and went off in search of leaves that I could use for rubbings.

I explored the plants around the lawn. The lavender leaves were too small and soft; the ginger plant was better: bigger and stronger. The honeysuckle climbing the garden wall was as tempting as honey itself, and I trod through Mother's flowers to bury my nose in the heady scent.

With a handful of leaves I returned to the bench, where Mother was drinking coffee with Madame B. and eating the layer cake that she'd brought from town. Monty was sitting between them. Since his accident he mostly just crouched beside Mother having his ears tickled.

"Arthur!" said Madame B., and attempted to squeeze my cheeks and pinch my nose. I managed to dodge her by feigning interest in Mother's new shoes, which were sitting in a box on her lap.

"Bertie brought them from the post office. Wasn't that kind?" said Mother. "I've lost track of how many months it's been since I sent for them."

I took the coffee tray, loaded it with art materials and lay down in the centre of the lawn. Wind slapped against the palm trees – it sounded as if the leaves were giant sails of tarpaulin. Beyond the boundary wall the gardeners were singing in the fields.

I placed a ginger leaf on the tray, put a piece of paper over it and rubbed with a green crayon. The shape of the leaf began to show. I repeated this process several times until I had lots of leaves covering the page like the wallpaper in the hotel lounge. Then I opened my book to the diagram of the butterfly, and very carefully began copying it, section by section.

"How are you, Martha?" asked Madame B. as I drew the abdomen.

Mother told Madame B. that she hadn't been sleeping.

"What does Dr Sadler suggest?"

"A drink before bedtime," said Mother laughing, but Madame B. didn't join in.

"And Albert?"

Mother sipped her coffee and took a bite of cake before answering quietly: "Albert keeps his thoughts to himself."

"If I can help in any way," said Madame B., and she drank her coffee too. I could hear her swallow it down.

"What are you working on, Arthur?" asked Mother after she and Madame B. hadn't spoken for a while. I showed her the abdomen and the forewings. "Lovely," she said, before saying to Madame B.: "All he thinks about is butterflies. I can't take that book away from him."

"So long as he's happy," said Madame B., and Mother shrugged. After a long silence Madame B. added: "It must be hard, Martha. Very hard."

I wondered what Madame B. meant, but I was more interested in drawing the hindwings of the butterfly than listening closely. Mother said something about "the worry of bullying and isolation" and "what the long-term implications might be".

"Dr Sadler wonders if it's connected to his birth – we didn't get the chance to bond the way we should have done." Mother raised an eyebrow. "I have my doubts." She drank her coffee.

"Anyway, we won't get a definitive answer here, that's for sure," she said when Madame B. said nothing. "I think he'd be better cared for in London, but Albert doesn't agree."

"Give it time," said Madame B., and squeezed Mother's hand. With no idea of what they were talking about, I concentrated on perfecting the antennae.

They drank their coffee and ate their cake – I coloured in my butterfly.

* * *

After lunch, when Madame B. had gone, I collected my bug kit, which consisted of a magnifying glass and tweezers in an old ice-cream tub, from the back lobby.

"Arthur, what are you doing?" asked Mother as she and Monty came to join me in the garden again. I was busy looking for caterpillar eggs in the flowerbeds.

Fabrice followed – chin sagging, shoulders round, belly soft – in his crisp white jacket and black trousers. He had my jam jars on a tray and a pot of tea for Mother, who sat on her bench, placing Monty beside her.

"I hope you're not covered in dirt from crawling around in there," she called. My shorts were muddy, but some eggs on a buddleia leaf grabbed my attention. I extracted them with my tweezers, placed them in a jar and studied them with my magnifying glass. They weren't quite white or brown – a bit like me. Eggs stood out against the leaves and dark soil, just as I did next to the local boys.

"Where's my boy?" asked Father, returning from the city. He kissed Mother on the cheek, rubbed his nose on Monty's muzzle, then came over to ruffle my hair.

"Those look like fine specimens," he said. "I'm not sure I've seen anything better in the lab." He took a good look before moving to the bench where he reclined – arms stretched along its back, his long legs placed out in front of him. He moved his Panama hat forward to shield his eyes.

It was then that a surprise discovery – a symmetrical cluster of pearly eggs on the silvery underside of a leaf

– made me start with excitement. I was certain that this was a cluster of *Charaxes acræoides* eggs – one of the rarest butterflies in Rwanda. A butterfly that had both the colour and stripes of a tiger, the spots of a cheetah and could fly just as fast as a tiger could run.

"What have you found?" Father asked.

I put down my jar, ran to the lawn, grabbed my book and went straight back into the flowerbed where I flicked quickly through the pages to confirm my find. My eyes darted between page and foliage.

Father laughed his big, booming laugh. Mother sighed.

Over the year I'd memorized every butterfly, learnt how to recognize different eggs and remembered all of their gestation periods. *African Butterflies* had taught me the correct temperature at which to keep them and the right amount of light too. I could tell when particular eggs would hatch into wriggling caterpillars and then eat their shells. But after a year I had still to learn how to keep the caterpillars alive and see them change into chrysalis and butterflies. That took greater patience than I was capable of at six years old.

"What have you got?" Father asked again, joining me in the undergrowth. "Can you tell me?" I wanted to tell him, I really did. I fought to say something, but all I could manage was to point at the picture of the *Charaxes acræoides* and then at the underside of the leaf. "Well, that's quite something," he said, hunching down beside me and inspecting my find. "*Charaxes acræoides* – tough to say, no?" I knew Father wanted me to try, but I couldn't. "It's not every day you see that. Sometime I'll have to take you up to the crater on the top of Mount Visoke. Up there butterflies fly in clouds around a lake." Father really should have said "rabble", which my book said was the collective noun for butterflies. He looked at me with bright eyes and ruffled my hair. "You're becoming quite the expert. Perhaps one day you'll work for me in the lab." He handed me a fresh jar and returned to his bench, where he stretched out again.

The thought of working with Father in the laboratory was almost as pleasant as the thought of working in the post office. Father was a doctor. Not a normal doctor – not like Dr Sadler. Father was a lab doctor – a doctor who treated monkeys as well as humans.

"Arthur," called Mother after I'd placed the eggs into the jar with the host buddleia leaves and screwed the lid back on tight. "Time for your story."

I used to think Mother loved Father's stories almost as much as me.

"Once upon a time, about a hundred years ago," Father began, taking off his hat and placing it on my head, "there was a powerful king called Kigeli IV Rwabugiri. He was treated like a god, and any man who tried to turn against him was killed, and their testicles hung on his sacred drum!"

Father winced, then chuckled. I didn't understand why: the King sounded very frightening to me.

Listening to the story, I turned to the *Charaxes acræoides* page of my book and drew a picture of my cluster of eggs in the space below the description of the butterfly and the diagrams of its egg, caterpillar and chrysalis. My picture didn't look much like the one in the book, but I was pleased with it nonetheless.

"The King was a tall, good-looking man with a long, golden headdress like a lion's mane. But he was harsh and made the Hutus poor and the Tutsis rich and powerful. He was also old, Arthur," said Father dreamily, "and soon he died, leaving many wives and many more children." I was glad to hear that the King had died: he sounded like a rotten villain to me. "Before he died he decided he wanted his son, Rutarindwa, to succeed him. The old King picked one of his wives, Kanjogera, to become the Queen Mother, even though she wasn't Rutarindwa's mother at all. But Kanjogera was wicked and, with her brother Kabera, they decided to kill the new King." I wiggled my tooth in excitement and imagined Kanjogera in black robes with no teeth, like the wicked queen I'd read about in my storybook. "After a bloody battle the King and his supporters were killed, and the Queen Mother immediately announced her own son, Musinga, as King." Father paused to let out a big yawn. "And just as *he* was being crowned, the Germans arrived." Father laughed, and Mother did too. I liked to hear them laugh together: it didn't happen often enough. "The Germans didn't understand that the Queen Mother was bad, so they let her do as she wished. She favoured the Tutsis and suppressed the Hutus even more, and in letting her do so the Germans created an explosive situation. And *that* is definitely a story for another day," said Father, taking his hat from my head and spinning it on a finger.

I wanted him to continue, but Mother was already collecting our things and talking about dinner and bed, saying, "The quicker you go to sleep, the sooner your birthday will come." And at six years old, soon to be seven, the excitement of a birthday exceeded everything else, including Father's story and my *Charaxes acræoides* eggs.

5

The following day I folded back my blanket as the cockerel crowed, reached under the bed and pulled out the jam pot to examine my eggs. Overnight, condensation had formed inside the jar, and the fine beads of water made it difficult to see. I gave it a gentle shake, flicked my fingernail against the glass and looked at it from every angle. The eggs were ever so slightly bigger than they'd been the day before.

At twenty past six Joseph whistled his way through the front garden – I moved the jar to the window sill for warmth, then went to the kitchen to fetch my two small green bananas and to feed Monty.

In the middle of the kitchen table, under a see-through cloche, was my birthday cake. I lifted the cloche and stood salivating like Monty on a hot day. It was a chocolate cake – delicious and gooey and all mine. Mother must have made it – cake being the only thing she could make. Fabrice only knew how to bake cookies.

"Happy birthday, Arthur," said Mother, appearing in the doorway. Her hair wasn't brushed, and there were pillow marks on her face. She had no colour to her skin and big grey rings circled her eyes. I wondered if she'd been up all night baking.

"How does it feel to be seven?"

I thought it would feel different being seven. I had hoped that being seven would feel better than being six. But it didn't. It felt just the same. I shrugged.

"Well, no cake until supper time," she said, filling up the kettle, her hands shaking. "Just because it's your birthday doesn't excuse you from your studies and chores. Now run along. Sebazungu will be waiting." I knew better than to delay when Mother was tired, so I retreated out of the kitchen. Upsetting Mother in the morning meant she could be in a mood for the rest of the day – and nobody wanted that.

I fed Monty, rode my trike once round the yard, took my bath, checked on my eggs and put on my green shorts and orange T-shirt – the clothes I wore every Thursday. At eight o'clock I opened the back door to head out to see Sebazungu, but a sudden blast of noise stopped me. I shut the door and rubbed my knuckles together.

"Arthur, for Heaven's sake," said Mother from behind me. "It's only the gardeners' wives and their babies." She might as well have said, "It's only a herd of stampeding elephants and their hungry calves," such was the fear the gardeners' wives invoked in me. They came to the back door on Thursday mornings for medicine. Mother was a botanist, but that was good enough for them. Father used to laugh about it. He called her the White Witch, a name I didn't like. It reminded me of the witch in the forest and the stampeding elephants that could return at any moment.

The gardeners didn't believe in visiting the doctor the same way Mother did. They believed in spells. I'd heard them talk about spells to make women fall in love with men, others to make women pregnant and others still to heal sick babies. Dr Sadler used to tut about it when babies were brought to him too sick to cure. The gardeners buried a baby most months.

"They don't bite," Mother said, but I couldn't be certain. She opened the door, and the women surged forward in one enormous herd. Even Monty cowered in the corner.

I took a deep breath, sneaked through the women's legs and only released my breath when I was through and clear and able to view the scene from the safety of the gate to the cutting shed and fields. More than twenty women gathered round the door, most of them clutching a screaming baby, with others strapped to their backs. They talked at Mother like bees buzzing round a tree hive. I don't know why: Mother didn't understand Kinyarwanda – she refused to learn anything other than greetings.

I left the women and the noise behind and went to the shack by the cutting shed where Sebazungu had his office.

The office was made from mud bricks and had a drape instead of a door, a small window with stained net curtains, a wobbly table (one leg was propped up by a piece of folded cardboard) and a filing cabinet that screeched every time it was opened and closed. I hated that noise.

"Arthur," said Sebazungu when I entered the office. "*Amakuru?*" I shuffled my feet on the dirt floor to indicate that I was fine and stuffed my hands into my pockets.

"*Quoi?*" he said, laughing. "Seven years old and still no tongue! But I told Mama Ruku this morning that I was certain you'd be getting a tongue today." I didn't like Sebazungu talking to his wife about me or teasing me about being mute. When he did, I felt awkward, aware that not talking wasn't normal. It made me feel as if I was to blame – and that made it worse. I looked at my shoes.

"This morning you make baskets. No tongue needed for that," he said, and led me to the cutting shed. Basket-making was awful: it made my fingers sore and my bum numb from sitting all morning on a hard stool. It was almost as bad as eating cabbage or going to the dentist.

I took a seat between the head gardener, Simon, who was stocky and walked with a swagger, and Thomas, the tallest gardener, who was gaunt and chewed tobacco.

Even though it was only eight in the morning, the gardeners were already busy. Every day at six thirty they arrived from their tiny mud homes scattered over the terraced hills, some on ramshackle bikes, others on foot. They arrived at dawn and left at dusk.

"Ah-fuh," said Simon in his loud voice. "Ah-fuh" was how Simon pronounced my name: he was trying to learn

English. Mother said he'd been trying for years. "How you go?" I looked up at his big hat that shaded his leathery skin and hid his eyes. I shuffled my feet.

"Ah-huh," he laughed. His breath made me turn away: it smelt as if his teeth were rotting. Mother said he had "halitosis – something he can't help", so I wasn't to make a fuss. It was difficult not to. He went about his basket-making, chanting loudly, "I am garden. I am garden," and breathing over everyone.

The gardeners chatted as they worked. Usually Sebazungu was there to translate for me, but that day he went off to do something else. I listened on my own, understanding snippets, but not enough.

"*U-u-umuzimu*," said Thomas, who was quietly spoken with a stutter. *Umuzimu* meant ghost. The others looked at me and laughed. I felt uneasy and wished Sebazungu would come back, or that Monty was with me. I thought the gardeners were making fun of my appearance.

I did look peculiar. Every time Mother and I went to town and I saw a *mzungu*, I thought how ghostly they seemed. They looked as if they might die from their greyness. I stared at them just as the gardeners stared at me. Where had we come from? Did England have no sun? Had all the rain Mother spoke about washed our colour away?

And I was thin, too thin – Dr Sadler said so. I was so thin I could play percussion on my ribs. It wasn't normal, not for a *mzungu*. White people were meant to be fat. I was odd. So I'd stare at myself too, I thought – but not on my birthday. I drifted into a world of butterfly eggs and chocolate cakes, which helped me to block out the gardeners' glances and ignore the pain of binding banana leaves to bamboo frames with raffia.

"*C'est ça*," said Simon, wiping his hands on his blue dungarees when the final basket was complete. "Lunch," he said, and the gardeners put down their things and went to the yard to eat the rice, cabbage and beans that Fabrice had prepared for them on the outside stove.

After I'd had a meal of pizza and jelly with Mother, I spent the rest of the day helping to make the bouquets. I stripped leaves from stems and sorted the flowers by type into buckets. Thomas and the others made up the bouquets, which were then checked by Simon and placed securely in a basket.

In the middle of the afternoon, when the gardeners stopped for milky tea, their wives, who had been sitting in the side garden all morning taking their medicine and feeding their babies, came to take the flowers away. It was their job to carry the flowers to the main road and put them on the bus to Kigali, where they would be taken to hotels, shops, embassies and the wives of foreign diplomats.

When the wives arrived, I rubbed my knuckles together and stayed out of the way, keeping a safe distance beside Joseph, who was back from his sleep and sawing firewood. He whistled as he worked – the gaps between his teeth made him an expert whistler. It was one of my favourite sounds.

"*Muraho*, Arthur," he said and gave me the thumbs up – the pad of his thumb had a deep scar. His gesture was the one he used to ask if I was OK. I gave a nod and watched him saw – I found the rhythm comforting. The wives lifted the baskets onto their heads and sang as they began the long walk to the road.

After they had gone and the work was done, the gardeners did as they did every Thursday: a game of draughts in the shed. I sat in the corner, out of the way, and watched Thomas stoop lazily to pick up the crate that had a chequerboard – eight by eight – painted on its base. He placed it in the centre of the cutting shed and rolled in two tree stumps that they used as stools. Simon threw contorted branches onto a blazing pyre, creating a woody smell of garden remains.

"Ah-fuh," he said, catching my eye. He held out his hand. I didn't take it, but I knelt beside him when he and Thomas sat down at the board. The gardeners crowded round.

Thomas took out the pieces – twenty-four used soda-bottle caps in black and red – from the pocket of his blazer, which was three sizes too big and covered in holes, and set them in place.

Simon handed me a coin, said "You" and flicked his fingers, which I understood to mean "You flip the coin". So I did. It landed head side up. Thomas clapped his hands in delight and some of the others cheered. He made the first move.

"Where?" asked Simon, looking from the board to me: I pointed to the piece I thought he should move. He slid it diagonally forward.

"Good choice," said Fabrice, arriving with cassava chips covered in salt for the gardeners. *Urwagwa*, banana beer, was passed round too. The gardeners supped on it slowly, wiping their mouths with the backs of their hands. Fabrice smiled at me reassuringly, then returned to the house to make dinner.

Thomas made his next move and Simon his, and soon I and everybody else was caught up in the game. Thomas leapt over Simon's pieces – Simon leapt over Thomas's. It wasn't long before each of them had several of the other's pieces and the cutting shed had come alive. It was warm from the fire and body heat; the scent of wood smoke and cassava rose to the rafters, and the place was filled with laughter as darkness crept in.

"Where?" asked Simon, and I saw an opportunity for him to reach the other end. I showed him the move. "Eh, Ah-fuh!" He laughed, his breath smelling of beer. "Very good."

He placed his piece on the opposite end of the board and requested Thomas crown his king. The gardeners whooped and drank their beers. Thomas laughed good-humouredly. Simon offered me a cassava chip to celebrate.

I chewed on the salty chip, while Thomas considered his play. He too found a way to reach the opposite end and casually held out his hand for a piece to crown his own king. Simon gave it grudgingly.

As the game became closer the anticipation grew. The gardeners jostled and bantered with every piece claimed. I wondered who would win. The tension built, the laughter heightened. Everyone was having fun. Just when things were really getting really good, Mother turned up.

"There you are, Arthur," she said, and picked her way through the gardeners, who pulled themselves upright, put down their beers and stopped their banter and laughter.

"It's time for your birthday tea." She held out her hand.

The pyre had begun to die down; the cassava and banana beer had all been consumed. Reluctantly I got up and took her hand.

"*Mwiriwe*," slurred the gardeners as she led me away.

"*Mwiriwe*," I said internally, wishing I could stay.

I never found out who won.

* * *

"Happy birthday, Son," said Father, ruffling my hair and kissing Mother on the top of her head instead of her cheek. We sat down at the dining-room table, with Monty curled at Mother's feet. "Have you had a good day? Can you tell me something about it?"

I thought about the boring hours of basket-making, the excitement of draughts, and then about my eggs and how they appeared to have grown. I fetched them for Father to see.

"Very good, Arthur. Very good indeed," he said with a smile, though I knew he was disappointed I'd shown him rather than told him. I placed my eggs on the table and let Father hold my hand.

Now that I was seven I thought I might have grown like my eggs. I stretched my heels towards the floor to see if they'd touch the antelope skin. They didn't. I slid forward in my seat, wondering how far I'd have to slide before I felt both heels on the ground. I didn't get the chance to find out.

"Arthur, sit up," said Mother.

"Martha," whispered Father.

I scrambled back into position and flicked through *African Butterflies*, which wasn't usually allowed at the table. "A birthday treat," Mother had said.

"That looks like fine soup," said Father when Fabrice arrived. He beamed and ladled it into our bowls.

"Hmm," said Mother, taking a sip and laying down her spoon. "It's far too salty. I can't eat it."

Fabrice sidled out with his tail between his legs, like Monty.

"All the more for us," chuckled Father. He looked at me with a twinkle in his eye and slurped back his soup. "Soup-er!" he said, and we both laughed. Laughter didn't frighten me the way talking did. Laughter actually felt quite nice, like sneezing or coughing. But Mother didn't laugh: she poured herself some wine.

"Happy birthday, Arthur," she said, raising her glass to me.

"Happy birthday indeed," said Father, lifting his glass – and so I held mine up too, which felt part grown-up, part silly. I wondered if this was the moment when they would bring out my gift. Father pushed back his chair. A bubble of anticipation formed in my tummy. Fabrice returned to remove the soup plates. Father pulled his chair back in, and the bubble burst. I wished Fabrice would hurry up.

As we waited for Fabrice, Mother ran a finger round the rim of her wineglass. It sounded like a mosquito. Father moved his eyes comically round the room looking for the imaginary insect, then swatted his neck by his ear. Pretending he'd killed the bug he brought his closed hand forward and opened it to reveal not a mosquito, but a hundred-franc coin.

I was amazed. Even Mother looked impressed.

He gave me the coin.

That hundred-franc piece was the first coin I had ever owned. It was like treasure to me. I turned it in my hand during the entire meal – tilapia fish and mashed potato, which was my favourite food, second only to chocolate cake – scrutinizing every detail and warming the cold metal in my palm. It was almost as fascinating as my eggs.

"Drum roll please," said Father, as Fabrice prepared for the cake to be brought through. I was so excited and twisting my wobbly tooth so much I thought it might fall out at the table.

Fabrice switched off the light and placed the cake in front of me. He had arranged seven blue candles in the shape of a seven. I liked that: it was ordered.

"Blow out the candles," said Father.

I blew hard and got as close to the flames as I could without burning myself. After three puffs the candles went out. Crinkles of smoke curved in front of Mother's tired face, but she clapped her hands and smiled – Father and Fabrice did too.

"First cut," said Father, handing me a sharp knife once Fabrice had put the light back on.

"Careful," said Mother as I sunk the knife into the icing and brought the blade up covered in chocolate and crumbs. I wanted to run my finger along the blade and not waste a bit, but doing so would have upset Mother: I was only allowed to handle blunt knives.

Fabrice sliced up the cake, and Father gave him a piece. Father excused him, and he left for the night.

"Try not to gobble," Mother said as I tucked in. "You're like a prize turkey when it comes to cakes."

"Let him gobble if he wants to – birthdays only come once a year," said Father. She took a mouthful and ventured a smile of her own. Mother liked chocolate cake too.

"Once you're done, Arthur," said Father, "I'd like you to come and take a look at the car. I heard an odd sound on my way back from the city and I want to get to the bottom of it. An extra pair of ears would come in handy. Does that sound OK?"

I looked to Mother.

"Just this once," she said, taking some port. Father stroked her hand and tried to slide the glass away, but Mother wouldn't let him. I rubbed my coin with my sticky fingers and pressed it against a page of *African Butterflies*. A brown imprint of the coin became embossed on the page. It looked like an official stamp, like the one the postmaster used. A fine-looking stamp, I thought.

After I'd eaten two and a half slices of cake, Mother went for a lie-down, followed by Monty. Father gave me a piggyback out to the car, which was parked in front of the house.

"Other side," he said, when I reached to open the passenger door. My face must have looked puzzled, because Father explained: "Thought you'd like to try for yourself, how does that sound?" It dawned on me what he meant – driving the car must be my birthday treat – so I ran to the driver's side and clambered onto his knee.

"Key in the ignition," he said. I bent round the steering wheel to see where the key went in. "That's it. Now turn it clockwise." I turned the key and felt a great thrill as the car surged to life and the radio blared into the night air. "Now then, we'll need lights," continued Father as he turned down the radio and pointed to the switch that controlled the headlamps. I flicked the switch, and the hydrangea bushes turned instantly from black outlines to brilliant colour. It was incredible. "I'll do the pedals if you do the steering." Gingerly we set off down the lane that led to the gates and the orange road below. "Wonderful, Arthur," said Father as we cruised down the lane, "wonderful."

As we approached the gates, Sebazungu appeared in the headlights. He put out his hand like a policeman, urging us to stop. Father brought the car to a standstill and asked me to turn it off.

"I must have a word with Sebazungu," he said. I was disappointed to have to stop: driving the car with Father was the best thing ever, even better than my birthday coin. "Out you get," he said, and opened the driver's door. I slid off his lap onto the lane.

"*Mwiriwe*," said Father. Sebazungu shook Father's hand but didn't place his left hand on his right arm the way he usually did to show respect. He had his hand raised to his chest.

"Good evening, Doctor."

"Is everything OK?"

"It's my chest, Doctor," said Sebazungu. His voice sounded different: it was clipped and wooden, like the voices on the radio. "I can't get rid of this trouble. Can you help?"

"Well, Arthur," said Father. "What do you think?"

I nodded. Of course we must help Sebazungu. What would Mother say if we didn't?

"Perhaps you could help?" suggested Father, which was odd – but I went along with him just the same. "Ask Sebazungu to take a seat in the front of the car so we can look him over."

I looked up at Sebazungu, who loomed over me, waiting for me to speak. I motioned with my eyes between him and the passenger door.

"*Là?*" he asked, opening the door. I confirmed with a nod. I heard Father release a small despondent sigh.

Sebazungu sat on the passenger seat, stiff and upright, and I sat beside Father on the driver's seat.

"Undo your jacket please," said Father. I wanted to hide, uncertain of what Sebazungu was about to reveal. For one awful moment I thought his chest might be wide open and spurting blood.

"Well, what have we here?" said Father when Sebazungu unbuttoned his jacket. I shut my eyes tight, too frightened to look.

It sounded as if Sebazungu was whimpering. I knew it must be bad. Sebazungu was the strongest man I knew, stronger even than Father.

"Take a look, Arthur," said Father after he'd finished examining him. I tried to show Father I was brave by opening one eye just a peep, just enough to prove I wasn't scared, but not so much that I'd see the full extent of Sebazungu's insides. But what I saw through my scrunched-up eyes wasn't blood and guts after all. To my complete surprise, it was a puppy.

"Happy birthday, Son," said Father, ruffling my hair. I scooped up the soft, wriggling creature. Sebazungu smiled broadly. "I hope that being seven will be better than being six."

A hundred-franc coin, driving Father's car *and* a puppy! I wanted to tell Father that this was the best birthday present ever – no doubt about it. I let the small dog lick my face and fought desperately to say that being seven was definitely better than being six. But all that came out was a grunt.

6

"And don't let him out of the front gate," Mother called after me as I ran through the yard the next morning, scattering the chickens, with Romeo bounding at my heels. Mother had picked the name. "Romeo," she had said, "do you like it?" I did – it sounded strong – so I had nodded my agreement.

I was meant to be having my English lesson, but Mother had paperwork to do, so English had to wait. I grabbed one of Fabrice's tea towels from the drying lines that criss-crossed the yard and scampered down the side of the house to the front garden.

I trod on the lavender that edged the path as Romeo and I ran towards the road, where Monty was curled under his favourite bush. Put out by our playfulness, he got up and limped inside. I trailed the white tea towel behind me like a snake, sliding it from side to side, in and out of Mother's flowerbeds, teasing Romeo, who tumbled after it as if it were real. From time to time he was distracted by a bee or by the sting of a thistle in his soft pads, but a snap of the cloth in the air was all it took to get his attention again. He jumped and barked at the towel, thinking it was a bird, as we skipped up the middle path, past the roses and back towards our ivy-covered house. At one point his sharp little teeth caught in the fabric, and I carried him along in flight. Down the far path we tore, pushing past the azaleas and buddleia bushes that prickled my forearms and calves and tripped up Romeo. When he attempted to scrabble to his feet, his soft fawn body rolled like the bread dough I helped Fabrice make in the kitchen.

As we played, a cabbage butterfly flitted past my nose and landed on a blue delphinium. Stopping to examine its starchy-white wings, brown tips and spots, I took my eyes off Romeo. The butterfly looked like the tea towel now splattered with mud. I stood staring at it for a long time and wanted to touch its hairy body, but as I extended my index finger, it flew up, up, up into the rising haze, over the flower beds and away, beyond the open garden gate.

I looked around for Romeo. He wasn't there. I looked to one o'clock. No Romeo. Then two, three, four, five o'clock. No Romeo. I turned around to six, seven, eight, nine, ten. And then to eleven and back to twelve – but still no Romeo. I turned my birthday coin over and over in my pocket and wiggled my tooth, anxious to know where he'd gone. I had been staring at the butterfly for ages and knew that Romeo could be anywhere. I wanted to call "Romeo", but my teeth felt glued together and my jaw wired shut. The desire to shout was suffocating.

Fixing my eyes on the garden gate, I knew I had to be brave – I'd have to leave the garden and the plantation on my own.

Cautiously I looked up the road, and then down towards the ladies at the shops, and on towards the school. The sound of children playing felt like pins on my skin. There was no sign of Romeo. I checked the dirt for tracks, something Father had taught me to do. The marks of one large and four small pads with tiny nails dotted the road. I followed the prints that zigzagged the dirt, dodging a motorcycle laden with potato sacks bouncing down the road. The paw prints led to the grass verge, then disappeared. A cobra, the colour of an unripe banana, slithered into the undergrowth and out of sight. I remembered Father's warning about snakes and moved away, following the verge, until I picked up Romeo's tracks again near the shops.

It was then that a yelp sounded from behind the buildings. *Yip, yip. Yip.* Romeo! I stood for a moment until I saw the lady who sold bread become distracted by a customer. I sneaked past her and down the alley. Romeo was there – in the grasp of the fuel attendant's son. I rubbed my knuckles raw.

When the boy saw me, he dropped his head to one side and let his tongue fall loose, trying to look like a dead dog. He held Romeo by the scruff. I lurched forward to grab him, but he dangled him just out of reach.

"What is it, *Mzungu*," he said, making grunting sounds that were supposed to sound like me but didn't. "Say *please* and I'll give him back." He laughed, knowing that I couldn't.

Romeo whimpered quietly, and so did I. The fuel attendant's son tossed Romeo from one hand to the other as
if he were a ball. The more terror I showed and the more
I grunted to say something, the higher he threw him and
let him fall.

"Don't you want him, *Mzungu*? Don't you want to say
please?" Rage boiled inside me and gagged the words I
wanted to yell. "*Mzungu* can't talk. *Mzungu* can't talk,"
he chanted and spat at the floor. A glob of spit clung to
my shoe.

I stood my ground and thought of a plan. We were sand-
wiched between the mud shops and a rickety wooden fence.
There was nothing there except a discarded metal cooking
pot filled with water. Its lid lay propped against the fence.

I glanced at the pot a moment too long, causing the boy
to look at it too. He picked up the lid and waved it like a
shield, then tossed Romeo into the pan and closed the lid
shut.

Instinctively I ran to the pot and kicked it over. Romeo
came tumbling out with the water, drenched and splutter-
ing. Both the fuel attendant's son and I lunged towards him,
but he was faster than me. He picked him up by the tail
and held him like a dripping rag. Romeo yelped frantically.

"What you do, *Mzungu*?" he sneered. "What you do?"

Clutching nervously at my pockets, I felt the shape of my
hundred-franc coin. Suddenly I knew what to do. I pulled
out the coin and held it close enough for him to see, but

far enough away so he couldn't snatch it. I allowed what sun there was to catch its shiny surface. It glinted. The fuel attendant's son eyed it eagerly and started towards me. But if he wanted my coin, he'd have to give me Romeo. He wasn't having both.

At that moment I heard a pattering. Romeo, upside down, wet and shivering, was peeing on the boy's prize jacket. Furious, he dropped him on the ground, grabbed the coin from my hand and bolted past, knocking me against the wall. My mouth took the hit. Recovering myself I bent down to scoop up Romeo and noticed small splashes of blood on the ground. There among them was my tooth. I picked it up to examine it. I was surprised at the length of the root.

Putting the tooth in my pocket I sat down in the dirt and held Romeo close. His heartbeat pounded in unison with mine. I began to tremble. Romeo did too. I rolled up my T-shirt to dry him off. We both cried. He scrabbled towards my chin, his scratchy little claws catching in my top. I pushed him back, but he tried again. His tongue was eager to lick the salty tears and blood that smeared my face.

I wanted to say his name to comfort him, but when I leant in to try and whisper it in his ear I saw in the dark pools of his eyes the reflection of a tall figure looming above us. I turned my head to see who it was.

The glare of sunlight, shining directly behind the figure, obscured the face. All I could see was round shoulders and the outline of a loaf in a carrier bag. And shoes – shiny, red shoes that made me relax a little.

"Eh, Arthur," said Fabrice, crouching down beside us. His dark, gentle face came close to mine, but not too close. His shoes creaked. "How are you?' I showed him Romeo. "Eh," he laughed, "*un autre chien*," and tickled Romeo under his chin. "*Il est gentil, n'est-ce pas?*" I nodded my agreement, then clenched my teeth together to show Fabrice my tooth had come out. I grimaced like one of the gorillas I'd seen in Father's books.

"*Eh, félicitations!*" said Fabrice, and I showed him my tooth, which he admired. "*Bien.* We go home?"

I thought about Mother. She would be angry: I was strictly forbidden to leave the plantation alone. And I'd given away my birthday coin.

Fabrice offered me his hand, but I didn't reach out.

"It's OK, Arthur," he said, interlocking his warm fingers with mine. "I no tell."

We walked back to the plantation hand in hand. I clasped Romeo to my chest and walked in the shadow of Fabrice's long legs, avoiding the stares of the passers-by and concentrating all my thoughts on Romeo. I tried as hard as I could not to think about the fuel attendant's son and my lost birthday coin. But then I remembered – when you try not to think about elephants, elephants are all you can think about.

* * *

Fabrice took me to the kitchen and sat me down. *African Butterflies* was on the table – a drop of blood splashed onto the first page. He gave me a cup of tea and a saucer of milk for Romeo, then put on the radio and called, "Celeste."

I circled the hole in my gum with my tongue: the flesh was raw and loose. My mouth no longer felt like my own.

"OK, Arthur," said Fabrice, who had begun to wash potatoes at the sink.

Celeste hobbled into the kitchen. She looked at my dirty shorts and bloodstained T-shirt and sucked her teeth.

"What happen?" she asked. Celeste had a deep, resonating voice that had a calming effect. She only ever spoke in the present tense, which I thought was funny even then.

"His tooth," said Fabrice. I liked it when Fabrice answered for me; he did it a lot.

Celeste took a look and broke into her wide, gummy grin.

"Big boy now," she laughed, placing her hands on her wide hips. She disappeared, returning a few minutes later with a red T-shirt and brown shorts – my Saturday clothes. I twisted my lips and rubbed my knuckles some more.

"OK, Arthur," repeated Fabrice. "It's OK."

Celeste took me to the bathroom and gently mopped my mouth, making me rinse and spit. That done, I undressed and put on my fresh clothes, which felt wrong on a Friday:

there was nothing brown or red about Fridays – nothing at all. I took three deep breaths to stop my chest from bursting. Celeste fished my tooth out of my pocket, handed it to me and blotted the bloodstains on my clothes with cold water.

I went to my bedroom to check on the butterfly eggs, which looked darker than they'd been that morning. Wanting to fetch my bug kit to study them more closely, I ran to the back lobby, where Celeste was already scrubbing my shorts. She laughed as I climbed eagerly onto a stool to take my kit down from the shelf.

Running straight back to my bedroom I unscrewed the lid of the jam jar, prised out the leaf with the eggs and placed it on the window sill, where I could see it perfectly in the bright light. Kneeling down on the window seat, where Romeo had fallen asleep, I held the magnifying glass to my eye. I moved it backward and forward until I found the right focus on the eggs. The caterpillars had started to hatch.

Two pairs of front legs emerged from the eggs. They hauled and stretched their long bodies like Joseph wriggling out of his sleeping bag. Their transparent, black-and-orange bodies were like sticky jelly sweets. I wondered what they would taste like.

I stared at the tiny creatures until the midday sun was long gone from my window and Romeo had woken up. Their hairy little bodies darkened as they started devouring their egg casings, just as it was described in *African Butterflies*.

That was their first meal. I drew a picture of the caterpillars in my book, next to the one I'd done of the eggs.

Slipping the leaf and its new occupants back into the jar, I thought I'd need something bigger for them to live in. Something better, I decided – something without ragged edges like the punctured holes of the jam-pot lid. As I got up to find a new container, a figure moved in front of my window.

I hunkered down. Only my forehead could have been visible at the window. I scanned the garden. My eyes roamed from the lane to the buddleia bush, from the five front steps to the orange-coloured road. Monty was with Mother, Romeo with me. What I'd seen had been too small to be one of the gardeners, too big to be the house cat. I looked harder but saw nothing. When I eventually stood up, a figure scarpered out of the hydrangea and ran straight into the buddleia.

I threw myself away from the window and up against the wall. The fuel attendant's son, I thought, terrified he'd come back for Romeo.

After a very long time, and when I was certain he must be gone, I inched towards the window again. As my body twisted into the afternoon light, I could see the figure still hiding in the bush. My eyes scanned the shoeless feet and bare legs that looked like twigs. It wasn't the fuel attendant's son – he had been wearing long trousers.

Given that they were hiding in a buddleia, I reasoned, they couldn't be all that scary. I stepped in front of the window and saw the face of a girl, peering wide-eyed from within the bush. On seeing me, she took a step back and hid among the flowers.

7

The girl in the buddleia bush was troubling. I sat on the bed, held the jar of caterpillars in one hand and tickled Romeo's ear with the other. Had it not been for the girl in the bush I would have been quite content. But she worried me: her presence made me question whether even with Romeo and my newly hatched caterpillars there was still something missing in my life.

To calm myself I stared into the jam pot and remembered I needed something bigger and better for my new friends to live in. I'd need a container, a lid without ragged edges, some sticks and food. Caterpillars, I had learnt from *African Butterflies*, are very picky eaters. They will starve to death before eating the wrong thing. I left my bedroom and went to the pantry to see what I could find.

"Fabrice told me about your tooth," said Mother as I rummaged about looking for something to fill with sticks and leaves. She held my chin and had a good look inside my mouth. "Where is it?" I produced it from my pocket.

"Your first tooth," she said. I was surprised to see two big tears burst from her eyes, which she wiped away before taking a deep breath and placing the tooth in her own pocket. "And what are you doing?" I pointed to the jar that

I'd placed on the table. She gave a funny little smile and shook her head. "Just don't make a mess, whatever it is." Then she disappeared with Monty following behind her. My tooth had distracted Mother from my missing coin and my Saturday clothes. I was glad about that.

Finding nothing for my caterpillars on the shelves, I opened the fridge, where I found a gallon-sized container of orange juice. It was perfect, but still a quarter full. I took off the lid, gulped down the contents and immediately felt sick. Romeo seemed to cast me a knowing eye – the previous night he'd eaten hot mashed potato from the dinner table and thrown up on the laundry-room floor. Celeste hadn't been pleased – she wasn't that keen on dogs at the best of times: she said they were only good for killing rats and didn't understand how Mother could have them in the house.

"Careful, Arthur – you be sick," she said, coming in with a bucket of water.

I stumbled to the back door, jar and juice container in hand, and turned on the outside tap. The water shot into the container and out of the neck in a cold spray that splashed my face. Romeo jumped out of the way and watched from a distance, along with the chickens. I filled it to the very top, then let it slosh out in glugs. It was clean.

My body shook from the cold water and the quarter-gallon of orange juice churning in my belly. Bending over, I heaved the juice up, vomiting easily like Romeo. I examined the contents and turned on the tap, washing the sick away. It was only after it had disappeared and my head had stopped spinning that I noticed, by the gate to Mother's side garden, two skinny black legs – the buddleia girl.

I tried not to feel embarrassed about the girl having watched me throw up. More importantly, I needed twigs for the caterpillars to pupate. "Pupate" – I liked that word: I'd learnt it from my book.

After picking up my things I walked, head down, towards the woodshed, with Romeo following behind. The girl inched her way towards the back door. I went into the resin-filled shed and moved towards the back. From there I could see her without her seeing me. Romeo hunkered down and snapped at flies, apparently uninterested in the girl, but I watched her every step. She was against the back of the house, clinging to the kitchen wall. Sliding her way along, arms by her sides, she looked like a capital A.

I collected a fistful of sticks from the floor, then emerged from the dark of the woodshed and sat in the opening next to Romeo. Now the girl could see me and I could see her. She looked startled, like a gecko when you turn on the light.

Keeping her in view, I held up the juice bottle and angled the twigs to see which ones I could use. They had to fit snugly so that the caterpillars had something solid to cling on to. The girl crept closer towards the back door. Her spindly dark body in a bright-red dress made me think of Mother's crocosmia flowers.

Between where she stood and the door I spotted a hand-saw. "Just what I need" – I thought – "I can chop off the top of the container and cut the sticks down to size." I laid the jar, juice bottle and twigs on the ground and picked up the saw. I'd never held one before, but I'd seen Joseph saw plenty of things. I placed my hand firmly on the bottle and set about it. The vibrations tickled my arm but it worked. As the plastic shavings gathered on the ground I could feel the girl watching – her bare feet creeping closer. Her toenails were like the shells on the shore of Lake Kivu.

Eventually the top of the bottle dropped to one side and I was left with a neat-edged tub. I pushed the sticks at angles until they fitted perfectly. I was pleased.

All I needed to complete the job was foliage and a cover. I didn't like to leave the yard with the girl clinging to the wall, but Fabrice was in the kitchen listening to the radio and Celeste was washing floors. The girl couldn't get into the house without them noticing. I shot her a warning look, picked up my things and ran to the buddleia in the garden.

The buddleia was a bendy bush, difficult to break. Its lolly-shaped flowers smelt sweet as I tugged at the branches, which sprang back in a shimmer of purple. I grabbed a small branch and twisted: it came away with a ragged green cut. I felt as if I'd wounded it. I took another, then another, inspecting them for spiders – I didn't want my caterpillars to be eaten by predators. I placed them among the twigs in the container. I was proud of my work – silvery leaves and dark sticks – my very own caterpillar farm. It was good.

When I was done, I looked around to see where the girl might be. I glanced towards my bedroom window to check she wasn't there: she wasn't. Curiosity got the better of me and, after transferring the caterpillars from the jar to their new home, I went back to the house in search of a cheesecloth, an elastic band and – the girl.

"Eh, Arthur," said Fabrice as I looked for a cloth in the pantry. "That's nice, very nice," he said, admiring my farm. I secured a thick rubber band around a cheesecloth and the tub. He put his hands on his hips and smiled, saying: "Eh, I know someone who'd like that." I gave him a wary look. Why did he think I'd want to share my caterpillar colony? "Come to the kitchen," he said. "I show you how to clean it." This, I was aware, was a bribe. I knew about those. Sometimes Mother had to bribe the gardeners with banana beer to work harder.

I was about to put my caterpillar farm on the kitchen table, when I saw the buddleia girl standing at the sink. I tugged at Fabrice's trousers and shot a look in her direction.

"Eh, Arthur," he said, laughing, "it's OK. This is Benitha." The girl turned towards me: water from her hands dripped onto the floor. "Beni is my granddaughter."

We stared at each other – Fabrice busied himself, seeming not to notice our unease. I looked at Beni in her red dress, her skinny limbs, beaded hair and buddleia flower tucked behind her ear. Her eyes, which were bright like her face, were the shape and colour of almonds and, as she smiled, I noticed her new front teeth formed an upside-down V.

"What is it?" she asked shyly, looking at my farm. Before I could stop myself I placed the farm on the table for her to see.

"It's his caterpillar farm," said Fabrice.

I pointed to the leaf where my newly hatched caterpillars were clambering. She craned her neck and took a step away from the sink. I took a pace back.

"OK, Arthur," said Fabrice. "OK."

Beni knelt down and peered into the juice container. She tapped her finger against the side. I frowned. She started to turn the farm around. I reached out to stop her. She flinched. The flower behind her ear fell to the table.

"Eh," said Fabrice, as he finished washing the dishes Beni had abandoned. "Caterpillars have one job. It is what?" he asked triumphantly. The answer was "eating". I wondered if Beni knew too.

I wondered if she went to the school with the saggy-eyed teacher where Mother had taken me when I was five – and, if so, why she was here on Friday with Fabrice.

"To eat," said Fabrice, wiping his hands on the tea towel that hung from his belt. "And when they eat, then what?" he asked.

Beni giggled, covering her mouth with her fingers.

"What?" smiled Fabrice. "What?"

Beni giggled again: too shy to answer.

"Waste," said Fabrice. "Waste, waste, waste."

I wanted to tell them that caterpillar poop was called frass. I knew that because I had read it in my book, but I couldn't think of how to communicate it to them, so I just listened instead.

"We must clean every day. Every day," repeated Fabrice, stepping out of the kitchen. "Every day," I heard him say again in the pantry.

I knew that mould could grow if I didn't keep the farm clean. Did Beni know too? Had the teacher taught her that in school? She giggled as I pretended to study the caterpillars, but really I was studying her. I looked up – she looked down. She looked up – I looked down. I slipped the buddleia flower from across the table and into my pocket: I thought it would be nice to press.

Fabrice returned with Father's old newspapers, which he'd brought back from the city.

"*Et voilà*," he said, tearing off a sheet. "Put this on the bottom and change it every day. This will keep it clean. Now go and find a light space to keep them, but not in direct sunlight," he warned. "Caterpillars can die from too much heat."

* * *

Beni started to come to the house every Friday to help Fabrice. She'd wash dishes, peel potatoes and sift the rice while I studied English grammar with Mother. As the weeks passed and the dry season turned to wet, I grew to accept Beni with her almond eyes, V-shaped front teeth and twig-like legs. I got used to her dripping water over the kitchen floor, leaving potato peel in the yard and sitting with her legs wide open when sifting rice, so that I could see her underwear.

Beni always smiled. She skipped and ran everywhere, her beaded cornrows bouncing from side to side. When she first arrived I'd listen to her talk with Fabrice, whom she called *Sogokuru*, from the safety of the living room. I spent more time with my cars on the rug than I'd ever done in the past. It drove Mother crazy. I made more frequent trips to the pantry in search of food I didn't need, so that I might see what Beni was doing. And when I was feeling brave I'd go as far as the kitchen and stand in the door and watch her wash dishes from behind, her head swaying as she hummed a tune and played with the bubbles.

Of course, as soon as she turned around I'd run to the safety of my bedroom, where I knew she was not allowed to go. Beni had to remain in the kitchen, pantry and back lobby: the rest of the house was out of bounds.

But one day when I ran to my bedroom Beni didn't remain in the kitchen, the pantry or the back lobby: Beni crept through the living room and up the red-concrete corridor to my bedroom door.

She stared at me sitting on the floor with my caterpillar farm. But she didn't stare at me the way most people did – as if I were a ghoul, as if they might catch something. Beni stared at me as if my pale skin and straight hair were something nice, not ugly.

"Can I help?" she asked. I was placing new host leaves into the farm. The caterpillars were now fully grown, plump and greedy eaters. I had to give them food twice a day – and sometimes even that was not enough. They had grown so big they'd shed their old skins and eaten them, just as they'd eaten their eggs when they'd first hatched.

It was important to have clean hands when handling them – *African Butterflies* said so: caterpillars could easily become ill and die. I couldn't risk that. I looked at Beni's hands. Her fingers were like prunes, so I knew they were clean – clean from all the washing-up liquid and scrubbing.

Reaching under my bed I found a paintbrush and held it up to her. She checked over her shoulder and crossed my bedroom, took the brush from me and sat cross-legged on the floor. I tried hard not to look at her pale-yellow underpants.

African Butterflies was lying open at the page where I'd pressed the buddleia flower she'd been wearing the day we met. The page was stained with a sticky purple-and-yellow residue. She looked at the book and the flower. I closed it, avoiding her gaze.

94

I placed my paintbrush inside the farm and waited patiently for a caterpillar to move up and explore it. Beni watched what I did and copied me. She didn't ask questions, and I liked that. Silently we transferred all eleven caterpillars onto their new leaves. Then I removed the old leaves and placed them in the bin.

I'd turned my back on Beni for only a moment when she let out a squeal. She was squeezing the tip of her finger so hard it had turned purple. She reached it out to me, her eyes even wider than usual.

Beni had been pricked by a caterpillar spine. I knew it was harmless, but she didn't, so I took my tweezers from my bug kit and moved closer. I kept an arm's length away, but was close enough to smell her sweet milky breath, which reminded me of rice pudding. I took her pricked finger between my finger and thumb and brought it close to my face, examined the spine, clamped the tweezers around it and tugged. It came away effortlessly.

Beni examined her swollen finger, which wept a pinhead of blood. Our eyes met. I parted my lips, wanting to say something, but not sure what or how. For the first time in my life my fear of talking irked me. Before I could think of what to do she broke into a smile and left.

8

1988

Over a year passed before Beni and I managed to create the perfect environment for a caterpillar to change into a chrysalis. It wasn't until we'd found a sixth batch of eggs, waited almost two weeks for them to hatch and another three for them to shed their skins several times, that the final transformation eventually took place.

I was getting ready for bed one Friday evening when I noticed a caterpillar hanging from a twig, like a cone from a pine tree. I knew that particular caterpillar had already been through two instars – the phase between skin moults – and my book said there'd be a third. But when I looked the next morning, hanging from the twig wasn't a caterpillar but a shiny, speckled chrysalis. It was as glossy as one of Mother's silk scarves.

I was desperate to show it to Beni straight away, but I had to go through the morning routine: wait for Joseph to walk through the garden, eat my green bananas and feed the dogs.

At seven o'clock I washed and dressed – brown shorts and red T-shirt – with greater speed than usual. Then, very carefully, I transferred the chrysalis into a jar and placed it in my rucksack, together with my book and a pillow, so that the jar wouldn't move about on the walk to Beni's house.

In the pantry I took down an old biscuit tin and filled it with cheese, cold chicken and four slices of bread. I took two bottles of soda from the crate on the floor and stashed everything into my bag, clapped for Romeo and sneaked out of the back door.

There was nobody around as I strode down the side of the house, with Romeo at my heels, through the front garden and out of the gate. Celeste wasn't out sweeping. The radio wasn't on. I remembered it was the last Saturday morning of the month and that everyone was busy with *umuganda* – community service. Father said that *umuganda* had been happening since his papa first arrived in Rwanda and that everyone, by law, had to take part. He said, "It's good for morale."

I walked the short distance from home to Beni's house feeling quite brave and grown up, but also a little worried that someone might tell Mother. The ladies at the shop laughed and said, "*Bonjour*." Their shop was closed for the morning – they were cleaning the road instead. Romeo gave the alley a wide berth – and on we went, round the bend and past the school.

Beni's mud shack, with its tin roof, neat rows of potatoes and a machete glimmering in the sun, looked inviting to me. I hadn't been to her house before, but Mother had pointed it out on our trips to town. I sat down on a smooth stone by the curtained doorway and waited, careful to keep my rucksack upright and feeling the sharp ridge of my new tooth with my tongue.

"*Mwaramutse*," said a voice from behind me. I looked up, my hand shielding my eyes from the morning sun. A woman as tall as the doorway smiled down at me. She had eyes the same shape as Beni's – though hers were not so bright – and her two front teeth were also in the shape of an upside-down V.

"Arthur?" she said, trying out my name for the first time. It sounded awkward for her to say. I nodded. The woman parted the curtain behind her and showed me in. I got up, lifted Romeo and took him inside.

The house had two rooms. In the first, which was very small, there were two large armchairs with swirly patterns, three white plastic seats and a low wooden table jammed in the middle. I sat on the armchair with Romeo, my rucksack still on, my legs pressed against the table. A second room led off the first, but the woman shut the door before I could see anything other than an old mattress. The floor was made of dirt; the walls were rough and grey. It was dark.

She disappeared out back, where I could hear her clattering pans and shooing bleating goats and calling "Beni! Beni!" After a few moments, Beni appeared. When she saw me, she broke into a huge smile, which seemed to make the dark room light.

"Arthur." She giggled and sat down beside me on the same large chair. She tickled Romeo's ears. Her bare legs pressed against mine, but I didn't mind. I'd become used to Beni touching me: it felt different from everyone else.

"This is Mama," said Beni when her mother returned, bringing *ikivuguto*, fermented milk. It was meant to be a treat, but I hated it. Beni looked pleased that her mama had brought me some, and Mother had told me that if I was ever offered it in someone's home I had to drink it – "all of it". I smiled at Beni's mama and took a mouthful of the warm rich liquid. I tried to ignore the fact that it smelt just like the cow it had come from and forced a smile. It was thick and sour, fizzy and sweet – disgusting! Beni drank hers quickly and wound up with a funny milk moustache, which I pointed out to her. She rubbed it off and jumped up.

"Come," she said.

We tore out through the back door, past the outside kitchen and toilet and into the field behind her house, in which were a few skinny cattle. Romeo nipped at the ankle of one: it kicked out its hoof with no more interest than if it were flicking its tail at an annoying fly.

When we were some distance from the house, we stopped to rest. I took off my rucksack to show Beni what was inside.

"Eh!" she said, and her eyes lit up. "We go to forest?"

I didn't want Beni to know I was afraid of the forest, or that it was strictly out of bounds, so I nodded, and off we went.

We ran through a maze of trails that skirted the edge of the plantation and led past small farms. We ran past people hacking grass with scythes, trimming bushes and repairing roads. Children ran after us – children with bows and arrows made from eucalyptus and bamboo – children spinning battered hubcaps on sticks – children with jerry-cans full of water, wearing hats made out of maize bags. On and on we went, always climbing, until it felt as though we'd left the world behind.

My legs were heavy and my lungs burned when the forest began to rise above us. Behind it loomed Mount Visoke, home of the red-haired witch who still plagued my imagination.

"In here," said Beni at the edge of the forest, where we stood catching our breath. I rubbed my knuckles together, plucking up my courage.

Beni showed me a different way in, one that didn't involve climbing through a slimy lava tunnel and through gnarly *hagenia* trees. I heard Father say once that "*hagenia* trees look like nice, scruffy old men" – but to me they resembled stooped witches. Even the name sounded like a cackle.

But Beni's route into the forest had no witch-like trees. It was more of a meadowy path with silver eucalyptus leaves shimmering above us. There were *hypericum* trees with bright-yellow flowers and veronicas too, in lavender and white. It felt like a magical glade – as if it was our secret – and that felt good.

"Over here," she said, weaving deeper into the forest in her pink dress, a blaze of colour flickering through the darkening trees. The farther in we went the more it seemed like the home of the red-haired witch and the stampeding elephants.

Beni moved so fast I could barely keep up. She was nimble like a gazelle. I kept one eye on Romeo and scanned every inch of the forest floor for snares and traps and anything else that the witch might have put there. And I was trying to keep the jar in place. I wanted to call out to Beni to slow down – to tell her to stop and look – but, as always, nothing came out: nothing but the odd grunt that she couldn't hear as she kept running ahead.

"Arthur," she said, laughing, when she eventually stopped to let me catch up. "Hurry."

I pretended my rucksack was heavy and made my way towards her.

"Look," she said, and pointed to a far corner of the forest, where Romeo was rooting about. "The cave."

I squinted, but couldn't see a cave. I was glad of that. A cave in the forest sounded like the perfect place for a witch to lure someone like me and make sure he was never seen again.

"You see?" She got down on her knees and began to crawl through a tiny opening that looked to be no more than a burrow. Within seconds she had disappeared entirely, and Romeo had joined her. I rubbed my knuckles together, hard and fast.

"Arthur," she beckoned, her face appearing in the opening. "Come on!"

I crouched down, looked at the hole and then at my rucksack, and shook my head. It wouldn't fit. But Beni had other ideas.

"Take it off," she said, and I knew I had to do it. I handed her the rucksack with the greatest of care. Then it was my turn to go in.

On all fours I wriggled feet first through the opening. When my legs were part-way in, it became clear there was nothing beneath them. There was a drop. I lay down on my front and shimmied back until Beni told me to let go. I didn't want to. I didn't know how deep it was or how far I might fall. But for Beni I knew I had to be brave: I let go – I let myself fall. My feet hit the ground almost instantly.

I stood in the cave, adjusting my eyes to the dark. Romeo was busy sniffing around the bumpy floor. The entrance let in enough light for me to see that it was about the same size as the hut in the clearing. It was wide enough for two, not really for three, and about as deep as the log shed in the yard. When I reached up, I could feel hardened lava above my head. There was a warmth to the cave that surprised me – and a slight smell of ethanol too.

On one wall there was a ledge of volcanic rock that was just like a table. I laid out the contents of my rucksack – the chrysalis in the jar, my book and the picnic – and gave

Beni my pillow to sit on. She held up the jar to the light and admired the chrysalis, while I made sandwiches.

I gave Beni the bigger of the two sandwiches, which she savoured as if it was a special treat. Romeo snuffled the ground for crumbs. As I ate mine, I thought I heard the snap of a twig on the forest floor. A bubble of anxiety popped in my stomach – Romeo cocked an ear, then went back to searching the floor. I flipped the lid of a soda and handed it to Beni, who appeared not to have noticed the sound outside. She gulped down her soda and let out a burp.

I opened *African Butterflies* and began sketching the chrysalis next to the drawings I'd done of the egg and caterpillar. Then I drew a little map of the forest and marked the cave with a cross on the back inside cover.

"Witch lives there." Beni pointed at Mount Visoke. We could see the summit through the cave opening. I nodded and tried hard not to show my concern. "She poisons people," she said casually, as if it was an everyday occurrence.

This was new to me. I added poison to the mental list of other things I knew about the witch: snares, traps, caging and training wild animals, living alone, raging temper and wild red hair. In the dark of the cave the witch seemed even more real to me than in the safety of my bed. I put down my sandwich and swallowed hard.

"Mama say: witch shoot people near her house – once she killed man who try to free gorilla. She shoot him in leg so he cannot run, then poisoned him. Mama say: witch put him in cage. He died, alone, after three months."

Beni told the story with such conviction that I believed her. I believed anything of that witch after what she'd done to Monty. I felt a pool of hatred well in my belly, but it quickly disappeared when I heard another crack in the undergrowth. I darted a look at Beni. She darted one back. The quiet in the cave was unlike anything I had experienced before. I could hear blood whirring in my ears.

"Grrarghh…" A mighty roar sounded from outside the cave. Romeo yapped and yapped. I rubbed my knuckles together as hard as I could, but even that didn't suppress my fear.

"Grrarghh…" It sounded again, but this time something blocked the light of the opening. We were plunged into darkness. Romeo hunkered down. I fought hard not to be sick.

"Grrarghh…" It sounded one more time, and a creature bolted through the opening of the cave and landed in beside us. Beni let out a scream that ricocheted off the walls. The cry I wanted to release made me feel like my head might explode. Romeo cowered in the corner. In the confusion it took me a while to make out the features of a boy only a few years older than us, with bloodshot eyes and shark-like teeth.

Beni trembled like a snared animal. I stood my ground, but my heartbeat was as loud as a drum. Romeo edged forward, growling and baring his teeth.

"Eh," said the boy, paying no attention to the dog. "*C'est le mzungu et son papillon.*" He ran a finger slowly under Beni's chin; she pulled away. He picked up *African Butterflies*, examined it – his dirty fingers left prints on the cover – and put it in his pocket. I grunted in frustration, wanting my book.

"*Quoi?*" he said, grabbing my soda from the ledge and drinking it in one greedy gulp. I took a step towards him, trying to find the courage to fight for my book.

"*Et qu'est-ce?*" He moved away, picked up the jar with the chrysalis and held it to the light. "*Un in-sec-te.*"

As I was trying to figure out how to get my book and chrysalis, the boy unscrewed the lid of the jar and shook out the contents. He then tugged the chrysalis from the twig. Romeo leapt and yapped, but the boy kicked him away. Anger poured out of me as he squeezed the chrysalis between his big fingers. The pressure inside me felt so huge I thought I might erupt like Nyiragongo.

"*Mange-la!*" he said suddenly, and clamped his big, dirty hand round my head, trying to shove the chrysalis into my mouth. Romeo tugged at his trouser leg, but the boy kicked him loose. I pressed my lips together, hard. I tried to pull away, but he was much stronger than me, and despite all my resistance I felt the chrysalis being squashed against my lips – its mushy, sticky insides smeared over my mouth.

"Stop!" yelled Beni.

She raised her soda bottle and brought it down on his head. The boy's grip loosened, and he slipped to the floor, where he fell in a heap.

"Run!" said Beni, retrieving my book from his pocket. Without collecting the rest of our things we flung ourselves out of the cave – Beni, Romeo and me – onto the forest floor, and ran faster towards home than any of us had ever run before.

9

When we were back on the plantation and doing chores in the yard, Beni told me she knew of the boy. His name was Zach. He lived with his uncle and aunt – the fuel attendant and his wife – because his own parents were dead. Zach and the fuel attendant's son, whose real name was Sammy, were cousins. Zach had a job as a security guard – Beni didn't know where – and Sammy helped out at the petrol station. Her Mother had warned her about them both and told her to keep out of their way. We had learnt our lesson that day.

The next morning I attempted to hide the fact I'd abandoned my pillow in the cave by folding up my jacket and pulling my blanket over it. Thankfully, when Mother entered my room she didn't notice: she had other things on her mind.

"Do you want to see Sebazungu fell the tree for the hotel?" she asked. Rather than have her wait for an answer or stay in any longer than necessary, I left my room and headed outside.

We went up to the clearing to watch Sebazungu and the gardeners cut down the tree, which fell to the ground with a thud. Sebazungu stood with his saw held up to the sky and watched as the gardeners bound it in rope.

"Very good, Sebazungu," said Mother. "Mr Umuhoza will be pleased: it's the perfect size. Make sure it's on the pickup in fifteen minutes. Come on, Arthur – we're going to town."

She took my hand and led me down the side of the bright chrysanthemum fields, through the spotted foxgloves and the golden alstroemeria that rippled in the breeze. I turned to watch the gardeners lift the load onto their shoulders. The green tree and their dark legs looked like a gigantic caterpillar creeping down the hill.

"Arthur," said Mother, "go wash your face before we leave."

In the yard I splashed cold water over my face, grabbed a towel from the drying line and ran back to the cutting shed, where I watched the gardeners roll the tree into the pickup. The plant juddered, then gave in to the force of Simon, who was ordering Thomas to pull the elastic cords tighter.

"Are you ready, Arthur?" asked Mother when the tree was secure. Romeo leapt into the front, and I lifted Monty in beside us. I moved my butterfly book from the warm seat to the glove compartment, while Sebazungu and Simon got into the back beside the tree.

Mother turned the key – the engine spluttered but didn't start. She tried again several times. "Not today!" she said, pumping the clutch and thumping the steering wheel in frustration. It was Christmas Eve, and if the pickup broke down we wouldn't be able to get things for Christmas dinner. Eventually it started up, fumes belching out of the exhaust. We turned out of the plantation and down the road.

"Look, Arthur," said Mother after we'd driven past the school. "There's Beni's house. Give her a wave." I wondered if Beni was in school. I wondered if, unlike me, she'd told her mother that we'd been to the cave and been frightened off by the boy with the bloodshot eyes. I felt guilty that Mother didn't know. It felt like a lie – and that didn't seem right.

* * *

"Remember not to touch things," said Mother for the umpteenth time as we pulled into the car park of the Kivu Hotel. Sebazungu and Simon jumped out of the back, saw off the beggar and began undoing the elastic cords round the tree. They cut the rope, and the branches pinged back to life with a sweet smell of pine. Romeo yapped excitedly – Monty limped behind Mother.

"Madame," said Mr Umuhoza as we entered the hotel, placing his hand in the small of her back. "How are you?"

Mother gave her reply.

"And good to see you, Arthur." He reached out to ruffle my hair, but I ducked out of the way.

"Off you go," said Mother to me as Mr Umuhoza took her into the lounge. "Go find some butterflies or shells by the lake."

Even though two years had passed since the day I'd been mobbed by the local children, I still didn't like to be alone on the beach. Most Tuesdays, when Mother was having coffee, I'd sit next to her and read *African Butterflies*, hoping she'd share her cake. But that day she wanted to be alone, so I decided to sit by the pool instead. I knew there'd be cake for Christmas, so I didn't mind.

I walked round the side of the pool with Romeo, looking for a shady place to sit away from the watchful eyes of the tall thin women on the pool loungers, in their brightly coloured swimsuits smelling of talcum powder.

At the far side of the pool – where nobody could see me – I sat down under a palm tree with Romeo and opened my book. I was reading about the development of chrysalides when a white man, in shorts, socks, garters and sandals approached with one of the ladies in the swimsuits. She wore so much make-up I couldn't say how old she was, but her bottom was as big and firm as a melon, and she wore her hair like a pineapple on top of her head.

The man patted the lady's bottom and kissed her cheek, which prompted a teasing laugh. They had a whispered conversation, then he reached into his back pocket and took out lots of money. He handed it to her. She counted it and put it in her handbag. I returned to my book.

Later on, when a twinge of pain from my front tooth drew my attention away from my reading, I glanced up to see Sebazungu standing over the same lady. I wasn't sure why he was talking to her when he should have been putting up the Christmas tree. What happened next surprised me. Sebazungu raised his voice at the lady and bent over her in the same way he did when one of the gardeners did something wrong. The lady didn't seem frightened like the gardeners: her eyes were so mean that I thought she might punch him. But instead of punching him she opened her handbag and gave him the money.

Then Mr Umuhoza arrived and took Sebazungu into the bar, where the ladies couldn't see them but I could. I held my book up, pretending to read. I couldn't hear what they were saying, but I could see that Mr Umuhoza was angry. He kept pointing at the lady's money, which was really the white man's, and which Sebazungu held on to tightly.

I glanced over at Mother to gauge her reaction, but she was tapping her watch face and looking at me, which meant it was time to go.

* * *

"Just a quick trip to Goma," said Mother as we left the hotel car park. Mother had sent Simon to the market for supplies; Sebazungu was still with Mr Umuhoza. There was something different about her voice: it didn't sound the way it usually did after coffee and cake; it was tight.

At the border to Zaire I waited in the jeep with the dogs. It was as hot as Fabrice's stove. I kept Mother in view via the side mirror. She forced her way through a crowd of people huddled around the two-roomed customs building who were waving passports and other bits of paper. She went into the first of the rooms, where there was an officer with a big buffalo chest sitting behind a desk. Mother pulled a bottle from her bag and handed it to him alongside her paperwork, which he stamped without even looking at her passport. She came back to the pickup, turned the key, tutted when the engine didn't start immediately, then backed out towards the city.

I hated Goma. It was dirty and smelly, busy and loud. Everything looked as if it had been drawn in charcoal and then smudged out. Grey potholed roads, volcanic ash and hardened lava made it look like a giant scar on the face of a dead man. It gave me the creeps.

"We'll just pop in on Mr Patel," said Mother. Mr Patel was the dentist. We never popped in on Mr Patel. We only ever went for a reason.

Running my tongue round my mouth I thought about the day my first tooth had come out over a year ago. Since that day I'd lost many more, some to jam sandwiches, others to absent-minded twisting – but all had been replaced with big teeth pushing through. My big front tooth, unlike the others, had come through crooked and brown. It hurt when I ate and drank. That's why I was seeing Mr Patel. I didn't know why Mother had to pretend otherwise.

"Come on, Arthur," said Mother as she parked the pickup in the gravel that was neither road nor pavement.

As I got out, clutching my book, I saw a man with no legs hauling himself through the dirt on his knuckles, which were wrapped in rags. I could see the brown blood seeping through the grey fabric. I tried to imagine how much it hurt to heave yourself on bleeding fists and what it felt like to have no legs. But I couldn't.

The man looked at Mother, then at me, and grunted something I didn't understand, pleading with his eyes like the dogs did for dinner scraps. Mother looked straight ahead, her face blank: she must have seen him, but she ignored him. I didn't understand why she gave scraps to the dogs, but didn't give anything to the man with no legs.

She took my hand and marched me up to Mr Patel's practice. The alley to the surgery was dark and narrow and littered with excrement. It opened into a yard through screeching sheet-metal gates. On two sides a brick wall with coils of barbed wire and broken glass surrounded a patch of dirt where blades of grass tried but failed to grow. On the other two sides was Dr Patel's L-shaped clinic with its barred windows. There were no butterflies or flowers in the yard. I used to wonder if there was a single butterfly or flower in the whole of Goma. It seemed unlikely.

"Hurry up, Arthur, there's nothing to be afraid of," said Mother, and she guided me up the cracked cement path towards the clinic door. The dogs lay down in the shade of the veranda – we went inside.

A small TV, mounted on the wall, blared into the reception room, which was full of boxes packed with green envelopes. Pieces of cardboard stuck up, with capital letters on them from A to Z. Seeing things in alphabetical order usually made me feel calm, but not at Mr Patel's. Nothing could make me feel calm at Mr Patel's – not my photo album, my chrysalides, my book or rubbing my knuckles together.

"*Bonjour, Madame Baptiste,*" said the receptionist, a big woman whose white uniform was too tight. I could see the shape of her underwear and bits of bare flesh where the buttons strained. She checked her appointment book and smiled at me from behind her wooden desk: her eye tooth shone a brilliant gold.

"I'll be back for him in an hour," Mother whispered to the receptionist – as if I might not hear over the television – as if I might not notice she was leaving.

"Arthur," she said, "there's nothing to worry about. This lady is going to look after you for an hour while I do some shopping." She placed her hand on my shoulder and said: "You'll be fine."

I sat on a green plastic chair, folded my arms and bit my lip, trying hard not to cry. I opened *African Butterflies* and leant forward to check for Romeo, who was keeping a lazy guard by the door. Tears plopped from my eyes and wrinkled the pages. I blotted them with my palm.

The receptionist disappeared into the surgery. I looked at the clock and watched every noisy second tick by. She reappeared, smiling, as if that might make me feel better. She returned to her filing, humming as she did so.

"Arthur," she said, after I'd listened to the clock tick over three minutes, "the doctor see you now." She indicated to the door with the little brass plaque that read "Mr Patel", with a whole lot of letters after his name. I stalled. "*Allez, Arthur. Le docteur est très occupé.*"

I pushed the door open and entered the hot room, which smelt of warm rubber and cloves. The receptionist closed the door behind me.

"Take a seat," said Mr Patel.

I walked towards the huge chair with its overhead lamp, spittoon and rack of gleaming instruments. I clambered onto the hard chair, which reclined until I was lying facing the broken ceiling panels. Mr Patel snapped his rubber gloves and readjusted his mask, then brought down the lamp, blinding me. I heard him select an instrument from his rack.

"Open wide," he said, then forced his rubbery fingers into the corners of my mouth, shoving in two pieces of cotton. "Hmm," he muttered, as he dragged the hook around my mouth. "Yeesss," he said, and tapped on my brown front tooth.

A current of pain coursed round my jaw, up through my temples, and filled my skull. He removed his fingers, cotton wool and instrument from my mouth, clicked off the lamp and sat me up.

"Arthur," he said from behind his mask, his eyes boring through me. "I need to extract a tooth."

* * *

I'm not sure I ever quite forgave Mother for leaving me alone with the dentist. When she returned from shopping I was waiting in reception, my mouth still numb from the huge needle Mr Patel had stuck into my gum.

"Well, maybe the tooth fairy will come," Mother said lightly as we got into the truck.

She had placed a tarpaulin over her shopping in the back, which was odd: she only covered her shopping during the wet season, and we weren't expecting rain. I stared through the back window hoping I could see something, maybe something for Christmas, but Mother pulled at my T-shirt and said, "Sit still until the anaesthetic has worn off. You don't want to be sick."

When we got home, she told me to go for a lie-down, adding: "Remember to put your tooth under your pillow."

I put it under my folded jacket and fell fast asleep.

The next thing I knew it was Christmas morning. I checked under my jacket to see what the tooth fairy had brought. The disappointment of finding my tooth still there stung more than Mr Patel's syringe.

10

"Very smart, Arthur," said Father, who was wearing clothes similar to mine. Christmas clothes made me want to burst, even though they were almost the same colour as the clothes I wore every Sunday: brown and blue. My shirt collar pinched my neck, and the tie was so tight I thought I might choke. Celeste had ironed paper-sharp creases down my trousers – I felt like the chicken Fabrice had stuffed and bound the night before. I clutched my book to my chest.

"Only for an hour," said Father, ruffling my hair. We were standing by the Christmas tree, its lights dimmed by the sunlight streaming through the windows. I cast him a doubtful look, knowing church dragged on for much longer on Christmas Day. "Well, maybe a little more than an hour," he said with a smile. "Maybe two." I knew we'd be lucky to get out before three hours had passed. "Then we can get stuck into presents and lunch. Good, huh?"

"Shall we go?" said Mother. "We don't want to be late." I wondered why not; nobody else was ever on time for church. She tied a silk scarf round her neck that matched the dress that she was wearing – a very rare occasion. She appeared gentler than usual, prettier too. Father looked pleased and gave her a kiss on the mouth. Mother pursed her lips momentarily as if remembering something, then busied herself around me.

"It's important we show up," she said, dabbing her handkerchief on her tongue and rubbing it on the corner of my mouth. "We don't want people thinking we're complete heathens," she added, examining the big gap in my gum.

"We do after all live in a Christian country," replied Father.

"Hardly." She put her hanky into her purse and opened the front door. "If it weren't for the Belgians, we'd be living in a country of infidels."

"If it weren't for the Belgians we wouldn't be here at all."

"Well, wouldn't that be terrible?" muttered Mother, closing the door behind us.

On the walk to church, Father told me the story about how the Belgians had taken over Rwanda from the Germans nearly seventy years earlier. And he told me about his father, Papa.

"He came to Rwanda in the 1930s to study the Hutus and the Tutsis," Father said. I thought about my favourite picture of Papa in my photo album. He was a Belgian scientist – a smart-looking man with a straight back who wore shiny shoes and stiff collars. In the photograph he was fitting someone's head with a strange wooden contraption that looked as if it screwed into the actual skull. And in the background, other men were measuring noses with callipers and consulting a chart.

"The Tutsis," Father went on, "were very tall, with light skin and big heads. They'd been in Rwanda for six hundred years, herding cattle and ruling the kingdom. They were thought to be warriors from a far-off land – some even believed they came from the sky." I reached out to hold Father's large hand, the skin of which was the lightest brown. I wondered if he was a warrior from the sky too.

"The Hutus were short and dark, with smaller heads, and were here long before the Tutsis. They were hard workers, ordinary people who followed the powerful, superior Tutsis." I squeezed Father's hand, urging him to continue.

"Papa and his men decided that the Tutsis must have bigger brains in their big heads and therefore must be smarter than the Hutus. The Belgians favoured the Tutsis and gave them the good jobs. Then they gave everybody a card to say to which group they belonged." I noticed Mother was shaking her head.

"After Papa had finished measuring people's heads he came here, to the plantation, and that's where he met my mother, Immaculée." I couldn't remember seeing a picture of Immaculée in my album. As we passed the closed-up shops I thought she must be like one of the laughing ladies with the yellow eyes. "Papa said she was by far the prettiest of all the Tutsi girls. He decided to marry her, and six months later I was born." He gave me a poke in the ribs and pulled a funny face as if to say "whoopsee" – just as he did when I was younger and I spilt my milk. Mother laughed a little, so I did too, even though I didn't know why they were laughing.

"Turns out Papa and Immaculée didn't like each other much. They separated before I was three years old, and two years later she died giving birth to another Belgian man's child." Father was very matter-of-fact about the death of his mother. The thought of Mother dying made me sick with worry. She put her arm round my shoulder. "That's when I was sent to boarding school."

In my album there was a tattered picture of Father as a glum-looking boy in a woollen coat on a station platform. I couldn't tell if he was unhappy because his mother had died or because he was being sent away to school, or both. Whichever, it was clear from his tone that boarding school in England was not something to wish for. Looking into the empty schoolyard, as we walked past, I wondered if school in England was anything like school in Rwanda – did their schools smell like hen coops too?

"Papa told me, 'It will do you good.'" Father put on a voice that was supposed to sound like his Papa's and wagged his finger, which made me giggle. "I didn't like boarding school much, but it did do me good.

"When I was eighteen I went to Oxford, and after that I spent five years travelling round Africa." I thought about the old photographs of him standing tall and upright behind dead lions, slumped elephants and heavy buffalo, with squads of men in dirty vests and big helmets. I loved those pictures. Father looked happy.

"It was on a trip back to England that I met your Mother. Like Immaculée, she was by far the prettiest girl in town." Mother rolled her eyes, but smiled too. "I asked her to marry me after only a month." Father looked fondly at Mother, the same way he did in the photo of them cutting their wedding cake, in which his eyes sparkled. Mother looked down at me, her look both wistful and sad. "After saying our vows, eating some cake and having our photograph taken, we said goodbye to England and set sail for Africa." A glance up at Father's lean face, with its long nose and plump lips, told him not to stop, but as we passed Beni's house Mother discouraged him from continuing with a slight shake of her head.

"Well," said Father, changing the subject. "In the end, not only did the Belgians get rid of the Germans, they also got rid of King Musinga. He fought against the Belgians when they were fighting the Germans, so they didn't like him much. And he was naughty and wouldn't go to church!" I wished I were the King, so that I didn't have to go to church. "So the Belgians picked a new king, Musinga's son. People called him *Mwami w'abazungu*, 'King of the Whites', because he dressed in Western clothes, drove his own car and went to church." I liked the idea of a king driving around in a car. "And if the King goes to church," concluded Father as we arrived outside the plain red-brick building where lots of people were milling about, "so does everyone else."

"Yeesss," said Mother, as though she didn't believe him. "Let's go inside, Arthur." She ushered me through the crowd of brightly dressed women and men wearing shirts and ties.

At the entrance, Father stopped to greet Sebazungu and Simon, who were talking animatedly to the priest as if they were the best of friends. Simon placed his left hand on his own arm when he shook Father's hand. Sebazungu didn't.

"*Mwaramutse*," said one of the elders inside the entrance.

"Good morning," said Mother.

"*Mwaramutse*," he said again, this time to me. I stared past him into the huge, barn-like church that smelt of straw and dung. I heard Mother mutter an apology to the elder – the same thing she said to every stranger who didn't know I didn't talk, something about "going through a difficult phase" – which clearly wasn't the truth – and hurried me along. The tang of warm bodies rose towards the giant wooden cross that hung slantwise above the altar, which was covered in faded artificial flowers. The concrete walls and floors shimmered, and the ironwork around the plain glass windows was brown with rust.

Mother greeted everyone she knew: Celeste and her family – twelve of them in total, all with smiles as wide and gummy as hers – Thomas chewing on tobacco and Joseph half-asleep from being awake all night in the yard. Hundreds of eyes followed us as we walked to the front.

I felt uncomfortable in my long trousers. All the other boys wore shorts.

"There, Arthur." Mother motioned towards a wooden bench in front of Beni's family. Beni was in her shiny Sunday dress, and her hair had been newly braided. Mother greeted Beni's parents, who nodded politely. Her *mama* was sitting upright and proud, wearing her Sunday best; her *data* held on to his Bible, which had an ID card as a marker and a black leather case. I thought I'd like such a case for my butterfly book.

We sat down. The bench buckled beneath us. Father acknowledged Beni's family and thumbed his Bible. Mother studied the growing congregation, nodding when she caught someone's eye. I watched the musicians, who wore dirty anoraks, rubber boots and trousers that were too big and covered in mud. They were playing out of tune, and the shrill noise from the speakers hurt my ears.

A family of seven joined us on the bench. They shoved us along until our shoulders were curved forward and our arms crossed. We sat huddled like golden monkeys on a straining branch: it felt as if we might crash to the ground.

The choir began to sing. The men wore uniforms that were just like my Christmas clothes – blue shirts and beige trousers – and the women black T-shirts under their glittering *mushanana*, traditional dresses. They made gestures with their hands – placing them on their hearts to signify love, or on their cheeks to symbolize sleep, and they swayed in time with the music.

As the choir sang, Mother nodded at a passing family. It was the fuel attendant with his fat wife, Sammy and Zach, who wore a bandage round his head.

"Ha-ha," Beni whispered in my ear, and I giggled. Mother placed her hand on my knee to shush me.

When the choir finished, the priest rose. The sun crept behind a cloud, and the church lost its glimmer. Mother sat with an attentive face, nodding her head and clasping her hands, listening to the priest, who preached in Kinyarwanda.

"*Imana, Imana,*" he shouted, over and over. Mother kept bobbing her head, even though I was sure she didn't understand. Father turned to the passage in his English Bible that the Priest was preaching about – Ephesians 4:1–6.

Time passed, and the congregation began to fidget – mothers took their screaming babies to the back of the church, fathers stifled yawns, children whispered messages, but the priest continued with his sermon. Father pointed to the relevant verse. "Be humble and gentle," it said. I became aware of the bones in my bottom. Beni swung her legs in boredom, her shoes kicked against our pew. Father nudged me and ran his finger along the words the preacher was quoting: "Keep the unity of the spirit through the bond of peace…"

The choir pretended to close their eyes in prayer, but really they were trying to sleep. But still the priest preached.

"There is one Lord, one faith, one God and Father who is over all and through all and in all…" I read, with Father's guidance.

The smell of bodies got worse. Little children ran outside and banged on the sheet-metal doors until their mothers let them in again. Even the elders, shuffling on the pews, rubbed their palms over their tired, hot faces.

Having lost interest in the sermon, I turned my attention to a shabby tiger moth, struggling along the dusty window ledge beside me. I scooped it up. Its wings fluttered gently, tickling my skin. Peeking through the hole in my cupped hands I blew on it lightly. It shut its wings defensively. I thought about how it would feel to pull them off. It was lethargic enough for me to try.

"Arthur," Mother rebuked me with a cross look, but there was a lightness in her expression that told me she understood. I placed the moth on an open page of my book, unharmed. Then the priest stared directly at our bench and shouted in English, thumping his Bible:

"The Devil is mighty, but God is *al*mighty."

He gave me such a fright that I slammed my book shut, squashing the moth to death. Beni smothered a giggle. The priest bowed his head in prayer. I opened my book to look at the moth: its yellow insides stained the page. I fell into an absence.

"Arthur," said Mother, tugging at my sleeve and bringing me round. The prayers were over, and she and Father were standing, waiting for me to join them. It was time for the collection. I squeezed past the family of seven and put our money in the small wooden box. An entire church of eyes watched me: everyone stared at the *mzungu* boy.

On our return Zach stuck his leg into the aisle. I tripped. Father caught me before I fell.

* * *

When we returned from church, Fabrice had already laid the table. Mother's crystal glasses were down from the shelves and sparkling, the silver cutlery was polished, the tablecloth was spotless, and in the centre was a flower arrangement with three candles. Fabrice had lit the fire, even though it was twenty-five degrees outside.

In my bedroom I took off my Christmas clothes and put on my brown shorts and blue T-shirt, which instantly made me feel better. I peered into my farm – the last remaining chrysalis clung inertly to a twig.

"Arthur. Dinner. Presents!" called Father from the living room.

Mother was lying on the sofa with a wineglass in her hand. Fabrice – who wore a cracker hat – was placing foie gras and toast on the table, while Father was busy under the tree.

"Dinner is served," said Fabrice, who stood to admire the table before returning to the kitchen.

"Foie gras?!" Mother asked Father as he spread it on his toast.

"It's Christmas, Martha," he replied, tucking in. "A treat."

"We could pay the staff's wages for a month with what that cost," she muttered, and took a swig of wine.

I nibbled a corner of foie gras and toast. It tasted like something Romeo would eat, so I fed it to him under the table – even he looked at it twice.

Mother rang the brass bell for Fabrice. We sat in silence, waiting for him. Mother drank her wine.

"Pull, Arthur," Father said, waving a shiny red cracker. I tugged hard. It gave way with a subdued bang. I put on the hat, read the joke to myself and put the small bag of tiddlywinks into the pocket of my shorts.

"Sorry I couldn't find a turkey," said Father when Fabrice returned with a roast chicken. He made a gobble sound and flapped his arms. "Gobble, gobble, Arthur. Can you say gobble?" I felt guilty when Father encouraged me to talk with humour. I wanted to say gobble for him but couldn't. It was as though my teeth were stuck together. Father looked discouraged, and that made me feel worse. I wished Father could be more like Mother, just ask a question and let it go.

Mother picked at her chicken; Father and I wolfed it down, scraping our plates and smiling at Fabrice when he gathered them up. I wondered if Beni was also having a Christmas – and, if so, with whom. Would she wait for her *sogokuru* to return home, or were they eating without him?

By the time Fabrice had returned with the pineapple cake that Father had brought from the city, Mother had moved back to the sofa with a glass of liqueur, and she soon fell asleep.

"Never mind, Arthur," said Father, when he saw me hover despondently between Mother and the presents under the tree. "We can open those ones later. Let's have a bit of fresh air."

He took me to the back yard, where a shiny new bike was waiting for me. Mother must have collected it from Goma.

The rubber handlebar was warm from the sun, and the letters BMX were emblazoned on the crossbar in yellow and white. I ran my hand over the saddle and stood back for a moment, then swung my leg over the bar and wriggled onto the seat. It felt good, softer than the trike – and higher too. My toes just about grazed the ground. Father put his hand on my back and encouraged me forward.

"Let's walk Fabrice home," he said, steering me down the path and onto the lane. I liked the idea: I could show Beni my new bike.

Off we went down the orange road – Father, Fabrice, Romeo and me. Father continued to steer, and Fabrice helped whenever I wobbled. Romeo ran alongside.

"Fabrice," said Father. I concentrated on the road. "I was telling Arthur this morning about King Rudahigwa."

"Eh, *Bwana*," said Fabrice, laughing. "King of Whites!"

"But not so white in the end, right?"

"No, *Bwana*," Fabrice tutted. "No, no, no. The King thinks *abazungu* like the Hutus too much."

"And was he right?" Father asked, placing his hand securely on my back and pulling me straight as the bike leant to one side.

"Yes, *Bwana*. *Abazungu* begin to help the Hutus."

"And the King didn't like the Whites helping the Hutus?"

"No, *Bwana*. The King want rid of *e-ve-ry Ab-a-zun-gu* so Tutsis can stay in power."

"But it was too late, no? The Hutus had already organized new political parties."

"Eh, *Bwana*, it is true. Soon Hutus and Tutsis were enemies."

Going too fast I lost my footing, and a pedal clipped my ankle bone. Fabrice reached out to steady me, and I regained control.

"And then the King suddenly died," said Father. I felt bad about that: I liked the King who drove his own car.

"Yes," said Fabrice. "Big funeral for Rudahigwa. Everyone sawree for the King and angry at *abazungu*. *Abazungu* kill Rudahigwa!" Fabrice was serious, but Father laughed.

"Rudahigwa was greedy, Fabrice. He ate and drank himself to death." Fabrice didn't respond. I wasn't sure he believed Father. I wasn't sure I believed Father. How much did one man have to eat and drink to kill himself? I wondered, correcting the position of my shaky front wheel without Father's help.

"And Rudahigwa's half-brother was chosen as the next king."

"Eh, Kigeri the Fifth," said Fabrice. "Very young, tall and thin." I imagined the new king as a giraffe, with a long neck and spindly legs.

"Too young, perhaps," said Father.

"Too young," agreed Fabrice.

Fabrice and Father stopped their conversation when we were past the shops and looked in the direction of the bar. I noticed Sebazungu standing with a group of men drinking banana beer. I had become more confident, and when Father shouted "One – two – three" and his hand came away from my back, I decided I could do it on my own. I rode towards the shack, showing off to Sebazungu, who was watching and laughing and pointing to all his friends to look at me on my new bike. Then suddenly my front wheel hit a pothole, and though I fought hard to control it, the bike toppled and I tumbled to the ground.

A great roar of laughter echoed through the air. I lay stunned with my legs under the bike. Fabrice lifted it from me. Sebazungu came forward and held out his hand – I took it. He pulled me up, but his hand slipped and I fell back to the ground. The crowd laughed some more.

"Come on, Arthur," said Father, helping me up and brushing me down. "We'll try again another day."

Sebazungu handed a beer to one of the people in the jeering crowd. I had to look twice before realizing it was

Sammy, the fuel attendant's son. He looked much more grown up in the company of men than he had next to his parents in church. Beside him was Zach. Sammy slapped him on the back and said:

"Eh, Zach. Look at the *mzungu*."

"Nice bike," he sneered.

"Arthur," said Father. "Come on. Let's go."

I took the bike from Fabrice and watched him walk slowly away, carrying his bag of Christmas scraps; every eye in the crowd followed him down the orange dirt road apart from Zach and Sammy, who kept their eyes on me.

Merry Christmas, Fabrice, I wanted to say. *Thank you.*

But the words remained buried within me.

11

Later that evening I heard the wheels of Father's car crunching down the lane. Sometimes he went out on an evening alone. I didn't know where he went or why, and I was always asleep by the time he got home. In the mornings, when I woke, he'd have left again for Kigali.

With Father gone and Mother in her room, I sat in my bedroom staring at the last remaining chrysalis. I studied it through my magnifying glass by the light of the fading bulb and the chugging sound of the generator. The chrysalis was dangling from a twig by the hook of its tail. I wondered when the metamorphosis would take place. I was desperate to see the transformation with my own eyes. My book said that it was "a very interesting event to witness, and everyone should make a point of watching it happen". I was determined not to miss it.

I pressed the magnifying glass as close to the chrysalis as I could. I was sure it began to move, almost imperceptibly. It seemed to vibrate. I was so excited I could barely hold the glass still. I wished Beni was with me.

Slowly the chrysalis's sides began to split, showing black and orange gashes similar to lava flow. The butterfly began to emerge, little by little. Small bursts of activity revealed more and more of its lacy, crumpled wings. As it slipped down further, there was a flare of orange and black.

Once free, the butterfly clung with its spidery legs to the remaining shell of the chrysalis. It tried to unfold its wings but failed, then tidied the remains of its cocoon. It remained attached to its old world until certain its wings would open.

I sat drawing the butterfly in my book, next to the picture of the egg, caterpillar and chrysalis. I drew its forewings striped with orange, black and tan, and then its orange hindwings, speckled with black.

I drew until I felt pins and needles in my calves. I unfolded my legs, and the butterfly fully unfolded her wings. I stood up, stretched and walked around the room, all the while watching the butterfly explore the caterpillar farm with her antennae.

Longing to show it to Beni, I took out an old jam jar from under my bed. I cupped my hands around the trembling butterfly and put it in the jar. Mother came in and stood at the window looking out over the front garden. Her cheeks were drained of colour. She came over to see what I was doing.

"What have you got there, Arthur?"

As I secured the lid, she told me in a faraway voice: "Catching them's the easy part: it's releasing them that's hard. You never know which way they're going to fly."

I didn't understand what she meant. I wanted to tell her about how many eggs Beni and I had collected over more than a year – and how few of those eggs had hatched into caterpillars and transformed into chrysalises – and that this was the only one that had made it to full adult stage. She must have known that releasing our butterfly wasn't hard at all – that was the easiest bit.

When Mother had returned to her bedroom, I pulled my jacket out from beneath my blanket, put it on and slipped the jar into my pocket. I opened the back door and stepped out into the dark, leaving the dogs behind and not even worrying about the mosquitoes. Joseph flashed his torch at me, and for a moment I stood in a circle of light. On seeing it was only me, he gave me the thumbs up, turned off the beam and hunkered into his sleeping bag, supping on the bottle of Primus that Mother had given him for Christmas.

I went to the log shed, collected my trike and tied it to the back of my new bike, then walked down the side of the house to the road. I rode with great care in the dark, past the closed-up shops and on towards the bar, where Sebazungu and the men were still gathered. They were huddled round a fire, drinking and smoking. It didn't smell like Father's cigarettes. They were shouting in Kinyarwanda, but spoke too quickly for me to understand. I hid in the shadows of the opposite shack and spied on them.

I recognized Simon by his big hat, Sammy and Zach, but it was too dark to make out anyone else.

Edging closer, I trod on a piece of wood that snapped beneath me. Sebazungu shot a look in my direction. I hunkered in the shadows and stood as still as possible.

He grabbed a flame torch and held it high. The other men turned quiet and stared out into the dark.

Unable to see me, Sebazungu returned to the gathering and took his place in the centre of the men, and the shouting began again. I inched away from the shack and crept through the dark down the side of the road.

When I arrived at Beni's house, there was no sign of her, just a few goats roaming about, neat rows of potatoes and the machete that shone in the moonlight. I leant the bikes against the side of the house and cupped my hands around my face, pressing my nose against the single glass pane. Beni, her *mama*, *data*, Fabrice and extended family – more people than I could count with the light of one candle – were huddled round the table eating a giant mound of food. They shared a fork and a spoon. It didn't look like the Christmas dinner we had eaten: it looked more like a mountain of cabbage and rice.

I tapped quietly at the window. Beni looked up. I tapped again and waved before ducking down. After a few moments she appeared from the back of the house. In the dark her eyes shone brighter than the moon.

"What you doing?" she whispered.

I showed her the butterfly in the jar. She gasped, then smiled.

"What to do?" she asked, and I pointed towards the crater, where I wanted to release it with all the other butterflies, which Father said "flew in clouds".

Beni frowned.

"It's dark – and far," she said.

I untied the trike and patted the seat.

After a moment's hesitation she got on and pedalled onto the road. I followed her three-wheel tracks towards the rocky road that led through the *shambas* and up to the forest.

When we passed the *shambas*, there were no children to follow us with hubcaps, jerrycans and sticks. Even the goats tethered at the side of the road paid little attention as we rode into the night.

We abandoned the bikes at the edge of the forest and entered by Beni's silvery glade. It twinkled in the moonlight like the diamonds I'd seen on tourists' hands at the hotel.

Creeping into the dense, dark forest, both of us picked our way through the twisted undergrowth and gnarly trunks. Every beat of a wing, snap of a twig or bird call made us pause to catch our breath. At last we found the gate that led to the path up the mountain. A sign hung from it that read:

DANGER

CRATER – DO NOT ENTER.

Ignoring the warning, I opened the gate and we started to climb. I scrabbled like three-legged Monty, one hand holding the jar in my pocket at all times, and Beni followed. We clambered on, grabbing at vines and tree roots, until the path became easier. On and on we went, through towering *hagenia* trees thick with damp lichen, dense bamboo and tall stinging nettles, until we reached a high plateau covered in clover and wild primroses. Long strands of lichen hung from branches, and orchids blossomed among the trees. Dotted about were little corrugated cabins hung with Christmas lights. The moon cast a soft glow on the clearing, as if this were the home of a fairy-tale princess.

From inside one of the cabins I heard singing and big, booming laughter. It sounded a lot like Father's laugh. Outside the cabin was a bath filled with a sweet-smelling brew. Washing lines criss-crossed the plateau. They were hung with socks and hiking boots that dangled by their laces – and there, beside them, was my rucksack and pillow. It dawned on me that this might be where the witch lived. Had she stolen my things from the cave? I pointed to show Beni. I could tell from her panicked expression – raised eyebrows and furrowed brow – that she was wondering the same.

I remembered the story of the witch and the man she had shot and poisoned, and was terrified she might do the same to us. Perhaps we would die a slow, painful death in a cage, without our parents knowing where we were. Suddenly I felt foolish for leaving Mother and the plantation on my own.

"This way," whispered Beni, and we crept round the camp boundary, tiptoeing nervously, desperate to get away. I was convinced we'd be killed if caught.

Just when I thought we'd made it, the door of the largest cabin was flown open. The witch stood in the doorway, wearing a black, loose robe. She was even taller than I remembered. Her mass of red hair seemed to burn like molten lava. She was holding a shotgun in her hands.

"What are you doing here?" she yelled when she got within range, the barrel of the gun pointing directly at us. "Who the hell are you?"

Beni tucked in behind me the way I used to hide behind Mother.

"You can't come in here, you'll frighten the gorillas!" she yelled.

I wondered why the witch would care about the gorillas she'd already snared and caged. Then she began to nod, laughed wickedly and pointed a knowing finger at me.

"You're Arthur, Albert's boy," she said, and I nodded.

"Well, well. So you've got a girlfriend." She laughed, and hot blood rose to my face. I moved a little to hide Beni from the witch. "Where are you headed?"

I pointed towards the crater at the top of the mountain. The witch shook her head.

"No, no – not tonight. It's too dangerous. Far too dangerous."

I guessed she meant the path was dangerous in the dark. I wanted to tell her we'd be fine: we just wanted to release our butterfly at the crater into a butterfly rabble.

"There are soldiers and poachers, Arthur," she said. "They wouldn't think twice about killing you or your little friend."

You're the poacher, I thought, straining every muscle in my neck to say something. Then a sudden noise from the other side of the camp distracted the witch, and Beni whispered: "Run!"

She grabbed my rucksack and pillow from the line, threw me the pillow and took off faster than a startled impala. I chased after her. We ran through thick undergrowth alongside a deep ravine that fell to a stony creek. Suddenly everything was cold and wet and slippery, and I was terrified that the jar and butterfly would fall from my pocket into the ravine below.

On and on we ran. Down, down, down through fierce stinging nettles and thick roots and mud. Down we ran, dangerously close to the ravine, grabbing at trees as we skidded on the slimy mud path. It took half the time to slide down the mountain than it had to climb up it. We made good progress until we reached the final steep descent that led back into the forest.

Beni's foot caught in the straps of the rucksack, and she toppled head first, rolling onto the ground below.

I skidded down the path after her on my buttocks, soiling my shorts with grass and mud, the jam jar rolling about in my pocket.

Beni stared up, frightened. She clutched her knee and moaned:

"It is bad."

I knew she wouldn't be able to walk or ride the trike home.

Seeing her lying there reminded me of the night in the forest when I was five years old. If I made it home that night, I thought, I can do the same again. I put the pillow in the rucksack, the pack on her and helped her onto my back. She was surprisingly heavy for a skinny girl.

Slowly we wound our way back through the trees. Beni barely spoke. She held on to me so tightly I had to loosen her grip to prevent her from strangling me. When we got to the silvery glade where we'd left our bikes, I felt exhausted: I was ready to crawl into bed and forget about the witch. Just a bike ride home, I told myself, as I put Beni down against a tree. I looked around for the bikes. But the bikes were gone.

"Maybe different tree?" suggested Beni, rubbing her knee.

I looked in the dark for ages.

"We took wrong path," she said despondently, but I noticed the bike tracks were still visible in the dirt. I rubbed my foot on them to show her that we were in the right place, then followed them for a while. They led off in a different direction to the route we had taken before. It was clear that they'd been stolen.

"We must walk," said Beni.

I knew there was no other way.

Limping down the track in the dark with me supporting Beni took a long time. Clouds covered the moon and, with no other light to guide us, every movement and sound was terrifying: a bird hoot was like a savage war cry, the outlines of trees like warriors and the blowing grass like legions of snakes. By the time I'd taken Beni home and reached the plantation, my chest was ready to explode.

Father's car was not in the drive. In the yard Joseph was snoring loudly, his empty beer bottle lying on the floor. I was glad he didn't see me without my bike, but cross that he was sleeping when he should have been guarding Mother and the house. Only Romeo stirred when I opened the back door: he glanced up from his bed, then curled his head back into his body. Monty snored louder than Joseph.

I slipped off my shoes, crept into the lounge and through to my bedroom. My feet were so damp I could tell, even in the dark, that they were leaving prints of moisture on the red concrete floor. I stopped outside Mother's room to see if she was awake. I pressed my ear against her door and held my breath. I couldn't hear anything, so I opened it. She was lying in bed with her eye mask on, snoring louder than Monty. I closed the door and breathed out. She obviously didn't know I'd gone up the mountain – nor did Father. Relieved, I took off my rucksack, put the butterfly back into its farm and went to bed.

Lying with my head on the pillow, I couldn't decide which part of the night had been the most frightening: hiding from the men at the bar, the encounter with the witch or having to walk back to the plantation alone after delivering Beni home. Thinking about that kept me awake for a long time, but still Father didn't return.

12

I woke the next day to the cockerel crowing and waited for Joseph to walk through the garden. Lying there I thought about my bike and how I wouldn't be able to ride it in the yard the way I'd ridden my trike every morning. And I thought about the butterfly too. Looking at it in its farm I imagined Beni and me at the crater releasing it among all the others. I was certain we'd get there soon.

After Joseph had passed my window, boots slapping, I got up, ate two small green bananas and fed the scraps to Romeo and Monty, then went outside. I sat in Joseph's lookout watching Celeste heat water and worried about Mother finding out about the bikes.

There was a faded picture of Celeste and Fabrice in my album that intrigued me. In the photo, taken outside the back door years before, Fabrice looked lean, upright and proud. He showed nothing of his round stomach, curved shoulders and sagging chin, but it was Celeste who had changed the most.

She stood with a serious expression – something all the workers did when they had their photograph taken. In the picture she was tall, slim and pretty, not like the woman I knew – the heavy old woman who walked hunched over a *fimbo*, was blind in one eye and looked as though the skin on the left side of her face had melted. The young Celeste had no cane, two good eyes and flawless skin. Father told me that Fabrice and Celeste had worked on the plantation since his papa had owned it, but he'd never said anything about what had happened to her.

When my watch read seven, Celeste picked up her buckets and gently motioned for me to follow. The prints on the floor and the dirt on my clothes must have led her to realize something was wrong. There was something in her gesture that told me she had figured out about the loss of the bikes and promised not to tell Mother.

In the bathroom I helped slosh the water into the tub, undressed and climbed in. Celeste broke away from her usual routine and sat in the chair beside me, where she kicked off her flip-flops and scratched the dry, hard skin of one foot with the toes of the other. She began to tell me a story.

"One night, when I is young, a Hutu leader is attacked," she said. "Hutus think: our leader is dead and violence fills Rwanda.

"Hutus attack Tutsis. They use spears, clubs, machetes and," she pretended to shoot a bow and arrow at me, which made me giggle, "anything dangerous. Soon Rwanda is chaos."

I tried to envisage the quiet hills and sleepy valleys around the plantation full of people fighting, but it was impossible. I rubbed a bar of soap over my ribcage.

"And one night, when clouds are low, Hutu neighbours attack my home. They burn roof and kill my cattle and beat me with club." Celeste glanced at her leg and raised her hand to her bad eye. I understood how her injuries came about.

"Your Father's papa save me. Arthur. He bring me here and hide me in cutting shed. He move cattle to forest and my things to house." She smiled faintly and paused.

"More cattle is killed, more buildings burnt, men dead in bananas groves and cornfields. Tutsis flee to Uganda and Belgian soldiers arrive. King Kigeri" – the one who looked like a giraffe, I thought – "drop paper from aeroplanes for fighting to stop. But Kigeri remain in palace and people get mad. The fighting, it last a month. Thousands without homes. Even more dead. Then Hutus take control." That last comment made Celeste suck her teeth.

The bath water was getting cold, but I was interested in her story, so I hugged my knees to keep warm a little longer.

"Hutu chiefs replace Tutsi chiefs and Tutsis leave Rwanda. Hutus take important jobs but…" She allowed herself a chuckle – her face looked entirely different when she smiled, her skin plumper, even the side that looked melted. "Hutus stupid, Arthur and Rwanda soon in trouble."

She gazed out the window with a distant look in her eye. It was hard to tell what she was thinking. Perhaps, I thought, she was thinking about her wounded cows or her friends lying dead among the cornfields. Perhaps she wondered how life might have been if it wasn't for the troubles.

"The church," she continued after a while, "they teach Hutu children: Tutsis are bad, different – from somewhere else." She pointed with a finger tipped with a thick yellow nail towards the sky, suggesting a mysterious, far-off planet. "Soon Hutus hate Tutsis and win first election."

Celeste, noticing me shivering, fetched my towel. She held it out, I got up, and she wrapped it round me snugly. She smelt comfortingly of wood smoke, from heating the water and doing the laundry.

"Kayibanda arrange coup," she said, and I allowed her to dry my hair gently, "and Sovereign Democratic Republic of Rwanda is declared. Hutus take control. Kayibanda is President and soon," she said, breaking into a full, mischievous grin, "*abazungu* leave too."

Celeste finished drying my hair and, though I didn't want it to be, I knew story time was over.

* * *

"Are you ready, Arthur?" said Mother. "We mustn't keep the Blanchetts waiting." I was investigating a colony of ants on the front step. They moved in patterns I didn't understand. I wanted to dip them in ink so that I could follow their tracks more easily, not go to the Blanchetts' for their New Year party.

"Come on then," said Father, folding up his newspaper. He'd been sitting in the car for ages waiting for Mother, who had taken longer than usual to put on her make-up.

I climbed into the back with my book and compared the picture of the *Charaxes acræoides* with my drawing. Mother stared out of the window. Father drove without speaking. I watched the world pass by.

When we arrived at the Blanchetts' house, Father sounded the horn at the gates and we waited for their security boy. I watched the sun fall over Lake Kivu. The sky looked like the layer cake Madame B. bought in town – bands of yellow and pink.

Eventually the metal gate clattered open, and we drove into the enormous compound. As if in slow motion we passed the security boy – it was Zach. Safe in the car I turned to watch him close the gate and run through the banana palms to his shack at the back of the house. We parked at the front, next to all the other cars.

"Martha, so good to see you," said Madame B., kissing the air by Mother's cheeks. Mother smiled.

"Come along, Arthur," said Mother, standing at the front door. I watched the peacocks parading across the front lawn.

"It's OK, Martha. He can come in later."

Mother and Father went into the house. I stood on the drive, clutching my book and staring at the prehistoric-looking legs of a peacock that strutted over the gravel, its blue-and-green feathers shining in the setting sun.

I followed it round the side of the house. From there I could see the whole of the tea plantation. As far as I could see, tea bushes streaked the terraced hills. I wandered after the peacock, his tail feathers tickling a trail in the dust, and followed him until he scrambled clumsily over a hedge and out of sight.

"Eh," said a voice from the boys' quarters – a row of corrugated tin shacks surrounded by banana palms. I stared into the dark. "Eh," said the voice, and a pebble shot past my foot. "You." The heavy "oo" made it sound big, as I imaged a gorilla would sound.

I turned towards the voice and saw two bloodshot eyes flashing out of the shack. It was Zach. My chest tightened. I checked behind me: there was no one else. He had to be talking to me.

"*Yego*," he said. "*Ici.*"

I walked towards him uncertainly, as if walking a tightrope.

"Come," he said, and I approached his hut.

He stepped back. I loitered at the entrance.

There was nothing in his shack apart from a sagging mattress on the floor, a string of damp clothes on a line and a cooking pot hanging from the ceiling. It smelt of sweat and cassava. The boy slugged from a brown bottle, then thrust it in my face. I didn't take it. He thrust it again.

This time I took the dirty bottle and wiped the rim. The fumes shot up my nostrils and irritated my throat. I sipped a tiny amount. The fiery liquid burned my mouth and strangled my windpipe, but somehow I managed to swallow, then coughed repeatedly. My eyes watered and stung, as if they might be bloodshot too.

I held out the bottle to him and wiped my mouth with the back of my hand, the way I'd seen the gardeners do after drinking beer. He didn't take it.

"*Plus!*" he said aggressively, and I took another swig.

Immediately my stomach burned, then my head turned dizzy and my vision blurred. The boy snatched back the bottle and took a gulp, which had no effect on him at all.

"*Comment t'appelles-tu, mzungu?*" he asked.

My hearing was now muted, my face flushed. I wondered if he'd poisoned me. I tried to run, but found I could only stagger.

"*Un peu plus,*" he said, but I wasn't going to take any more. I zigzagged from the shack as fast as my weakened legs would take me. I needed to find Mother.

"Eh," he called after me as I stumbled towards the house. "*Mzungu!*" He laughed barbarically – a sound that carried into the night.

* * *

When I opened the front door of the Blanchetts' house, a wave of sound and light hit me. Their entrance hall was as big as our living room, and they had cable electricity, not a generator like we did. The light in the house was even brighter than at the hotel. I squinted to stop it hurting my eyes.

The hall was full of adults talking loudly and laughing, drinking wine and eating nibbles from shiny silver trays. It smelt of salt and fish and cookies in the oven. There were three musicians in the corner, and waiters wove through the guests like dancers. The noise was too much: all the talking and laughing made my dizziness worse. I wanted to go home.

I couldn't see Mother anywhere. Or Father, for that matter. And I didn't recognize anyone. I held tightly to my book and wished Beni were there to keep me company. Snippets of conversation broke through the jumble of noise as I sneaked in and out of grown-ups' legs looking for my parents.

"Well, who have we here?" said a man when I stumbled into a group of people who were drinking dark-red wine that stained their lips. He bent down to within an inch from my face – I could smell the alcohol on his breath.

"If it's not Arthur Baptiste! How are the teeth?"

It took me a while to realize it was the dentist – I didn't recognize him without his mask. Fearful that he'd stick a needle in my mouth I backed away, but tripped over my own feet and fell in a heap on the floor.

"Arthur," said Mother, appearing above me. "What's the matter?"

"He's just had a fright," said the dentist.

Mother knelt down on the floor. She sniffed my lips, gave a quizzical look, then repeated the sniff.

"I don't think he's had a fright," she said after a moment's thought. "I think he's had a drink."

"Good lad!" said the dentist.

"I'm serious!" rebuked Mother.

The dentist sniffed my lips too.

"Smells like ethanol to me," he confirmed, and Mother frowned. "Take him through to a bedroom, Martha. He'll sleep it off."

Father arrived, and he and Mother took me to one of the Blanchetts' spare rooms. I couldn't tell what it looked like: Mother didn't turn on the light.

"Leave the door open just a crack," said Father as they left, but Mother eased the door shut: the only light in the room came from the small gap under the door.

Mother and Father went back to the party, and I listened to the distant laughter, the bass from the band and the popping of corks. I held on to *African Butterflies*, which was splattered with red wine. I wanted to wipe it off, but the paper had already soaked it up. I was about to fall asleep when approaching footsteps woke me.

"What's going on up in Kigali?' The voice sounded like Monsieur Blanchett's.

"Where do I start?" This was Father's. "Economic decline, corruption, rising unemployment and crime – the country's going to the dogs."

"And the assassination attempt?"

"Not sure, but he'd be wise to stay alert." I heard the sound of ice cubes in a glass. There was a pause.

"Damn country. Even the reliable staff are causing me trouble. Gates banging at all hours of the day and night. Don't know who's coming or going."

"We've had some trouble of our own," said Father. Their shoes broke the light under my door, and the sound of their wooden heels faded towards the party.

I wondered what Father had meant by "trouble of our own". Then I thought of my butterfly and of Beni and of what she might be doing. Was she also lying awake, trying to decipher grown-ups' talking while secretly thinking of me?

* * *

The day after the party, Father took me aside in the garden and told me seriously: "Arthur, I know you went up Mount Visoke, and I know you lost your bike."

I couldn't tell if he was disappointed or cross, or how he knew.

"If your Mother finds out, she'll be furious, so I want you to make a promise." I felt a nervous flutter in my stomach.

"I want you to promise never to go up the mountain again. Do you understand?"

I nodded, but tears welled in my eyes, and I fought to contain them. I wanted nothing more than to go to the crater to release my butterfly.

"If you don't go back, Arthur, I promise I won't tell Mother about your bike."

With my plans to return to the crater in tatters, I spent the next few months gazing longingly at the mountain, imagining great rabbles of butterflies flying round its top. It felt like the greatest sacrifice of my life not to be able to release the butterfly there.

As for the theft of the bikes, that went unspoken of until one Tuesday when Mother and I were in town. We were sitting in the pickup at the petrol station, waiting for the tank to be filled. I was trying to dodge the stares of Sammy, who was sitting with his fat mama husking corn in the shade, when Zach rode in on my bike. It was definitely mine: metallic blue shone in the sun and BMX was written in yellow and white on the crossbar. He rode it as if it had always been his. Mother and I stared at it as though this was the answer to a riddle we'd both been trying to solve for a very long time. I figured Father must have told her it had been stolen, which made me cross – I had kept my part of our promise.

Mother put down her soda and told me to stay in the truck. She opened her door and marched straight towards the boy.

"You! Little thief!" she shouted, then went right up to him and cuffed him round the ear. Zach, who was almost the same size as Mother, stumbled a little but recovered himself and squared up to her.

"Sebazungu!" called Mother – not that she needed to. Sebazungu, the fuel attendant and his son were already on their way to the scene. Even the fuel attendant's wife was hauling herself up from where she was seated.

Winding down my window I heard Mother say: "Ask this boy where he got that bike."

Sebazungu translated.

The boy, now cowering in the presence of the adults, said he took it from the forest. But Sebazungu told Mother, "He says it was a present from his uncle," and he motioned to the fuel attendant.

This confused me. I was certain about what the boy had said: my Kinyarwanda was getting much better.

Mother squinted at Sebazungu and then at Zach. She shook her head and muttered something before coming back to the truck. Zach shot a smug look in my direction.

"I thought it was yours," she told me. "But Sebazungu tells me differently."

I knew Mother wasn't certain. I wanted to tell her that Sebazungu hadn't told the truth, but I couldn't. I was angry with her for not learning Kinyarwanda and letting Sebazungu away with a lie, but I was even angrier with myself for not being able to say what I knew to be true.

Sebazungu returned to the truck and told Mother that if there was a missing bike he would talk to every worker on the plantation to find out what had happened. I tried not to catch his eye. I didn't want him to find out that I knew he'd lied to Mother.

13

1990

As far as I could tell, Sebazungu made no effort to talk to the gardeners and Mother did nothing more about the theft of my bike herself. Regardless, life continued on the plantation in much the same way as it had before. Small things changed, such as Father increasingly becoming distracted by the radio and newspapers. Occasionally I'd pick up his paper and read of a murdered politician, dead journalist or student shot at a protest. Father was not the only one who listened more to the radio. It was on constantly in the kitchen, where Fabrice and Celeste could listen, and Sebazungu hooked up a radio to a loudspeaker outside his office, so that the gardeners could hear it from where they were working in the fields.

From time to time Father would lose his temper with me – something he'd never done before. He spent days away in the city – which Mother reassured me was to do with "being very busy at work". But she told me in such a way that I felt she was hiding something or didn't know herself, which was worse than not being told at all.

With Father away for longer, Mother had more to do on the plantation and less time for my lessons, which meant

I had extra time to spend with Beni, who rarely went to school. Beni told me she missed her lessons with the schoolteacher; most days she worked in her family's field instead. When we could, we played in the garden with our butterfly, releasing it and catching it with the nets we made out of cane and old mosquito gauze. Beni often spoke about wanting to go back up the mountain again to release the butterfly; it frustrated me that I had no way of telling her that I was banned.

One Monday morning, when the sun was on the rise and the mist had cleared, Beni arrived at the back door. I was meant to be spending the day with the gardeners thinning saplings, but when Mother saw Beni she gave me permission to take the morning off, so long as I promised to play outside and keep out of her way. I fancied a game of hide-and-seek – a game much better suited to the outdoors than the confines of the house – so I was happy to oblige. The best place to play hide-and-seek wasn't in the yard or Mother's side garden, but out by the cutting shed, where there was much greater scope for places to hide.

Beni and I left the house and ran towards the shed; Romeo followed, and Monty stayed with Mother. Beni's cornrows bounced from side to side as she ran ahead of me. I figured that, wherever she chose to hide, I stood a good chance of finding her, given that the dress she was wearing was bright yellow.

At the cutting shed I indicated the game I wanted to play by covering my eyes and then revealing them again. Beni knew what I meant and quickly decided:

"You hide first."

I liked hiding much more than seeking, so with Beni counting in the corner I left the shed and headed into the field of golden alstroemeria, where the gardeners were thinning plants and listening to the radio. The voices from the radio carried to the back of the field and farther still; I found it hard to follow, such was the speed at which they spoke. Whatever was being said, it seemed to animate the gardeners, who were so busy bantering they did very little work. I hunkered down among the flower rows and shooed Romeo, so he wouldn't give my hiding place away. The pollen tickled my nose, and I tried hard not to sneeze. With my head peeking above the flowers, I watched Beni come round the side of the cutting shed and search the fields. She was like a bright dahlia with her dark limbs and yellow dress.

"Thomas," called Sebazungu. He was sitting on an upturned bucket chewing on sugar cane. Simon sat beside him, sharpening his machete.

Thomas looked up from where he was stooped over the saplings.

"Did you hear the President's speech?" Sebazungu asked in Kinyarwanda.

Thomas nodded and continued with his work.

"What did you think?"

Thomas shrugged his shoulders.

"Democracy," said Sebazungu, shaking his head and spitting out the sugar cane. "Habyarimana pleases no one in Rwanda." Simon nodded in agreement.

"M-m-maybe some," said Thomas, more to the flowers than to Sebazungu.

"*Quoi?*" Sebazungu sounded irritated. Thomas spat out his tobacco and repeated himself a little louder.

"Who?" Sebazungu laughed, and Simon did too. "You?"

"And others." Thomas looked at the gardeners around him. They were wearing different-coloured caps I hadn't noticed before. I liked the way they looked, bobbing brightly among the flowers.

Thomas reached into the pocket of his shabby blazer and produced a cap of his own. He pulled it on proudly. Sebazungu threw his sugar cane on the ground and got up, knocking over his bucket.

"Found you!" called Beni, crouching down beside me. I was so caught up in listening to what was going on that I'd completely forgotten about our game. I placed my finger to my lips, telling her to be quiet.

"Why?" she asked.

I pointed at Sebazungu, who was walking towards Thomas, ranting about something. Beni and I kept a look-out from between the flower stems.

"You understand what he say?" she asked.

I shook my head.

Beni listened and said:

"He is cross with President."

I furrowed my brow, uncertain why Sebazungu should be cross with someone he didn't know.

"He say: President pleases the West. President doesn't believe what he says."

Soon Sebazungu was standing next to Thomas attempting to snatch his cap, but Thomas stood perfectly upright so his cap was out of reach. Sebazungu continued to rant. Beni whispered:

"He say: you think President wants to share power? And Thomas say: President wants best for everyone."

Sebazungu laughed and laughed at Thomas. It didn't seem like nice laughter. I suspected he was laughing at Thomas the same way he'd laughed at me for being mute or falling off my bike. Thomas tried to talk back, but his stutter stopped him. Words stuck in the back of his throat. I knew exactly how that felt.

As Thomas choked on his words and Sebazungu goaded him, the radio suddenly cut off. Everyone stopped talking and turned to see what had happened.

Mother was striding through the field.

"No more radio," she shouted at the gardeners. "Back to work."

"No," Sebazungu protested. Simon looked pleased with himself, as if it were he who had refused Mother.

"I beg your pardon?" said Mother.

"These men must know what is happening to Rwanda."

"These men are paid to work!" At that moment no one was working, everyone was listening to Sebazungu and Mother arguing.

Sebazungu said: "You tell these men, 'Take off your caps or lose your jobs,' and I will turn off the radio."

"I'm not bargaining with you."

Sebazungu shrugged his shoulders casually and said, "Then the radio stays on."

Simon smirked, but stopped when Mother caught him.

After that Sebazungu and Mother stared at each other for what felt like a very long time. It was Mother who gave in first. She closed her eyes and released a long, slow breath that gave her the appearance of a wilting flower. Opening her eyes she told him, "Very well."

She turned to the gardeners and said, "Take off your caps," motioning what to do. "Those of you who don't needn't come back to work."

One by one the gardeners took off their caps and slipped them into their pockets. When every cap was removed and Sebazungu had gone back to work, Mother called briskly, "Arthur," and she looked around as if she was playing hide-and-seek too. I stood up from my place among the flowers. "That's enough for today. Time for Beni to go home." I didn't want her to go, and Beni's scrunched-up nose told me she didn't want to go either. But Mother would be in a bad mood if she didn't, so we walked through the field towards the house and garden. I had a sudden urge to hold Beni's hand.

"*Data* say President is good man," Beni said as we neared the road. "He say, life be better when changes come."

I wanted to hear about what the President was going to do, but before Beni could tell me more Mother called from the house: "Arthur, hurry up, it's time you did some school work."

Closing the gate, I watched Beni walk towards home and wondered about the changes to come.

14

"Gather round," said Father to the gardeners after church, which had been particularly dull that Sunday. I'd passed the time trying to memorize who was sitting where, like a giant version of Kim's Game. It was complicated by the fact that many of the people who usually sat next to each other had switched places.

In the side garden the gardeners were having lunch provided by Mother and Father, something that happened each week. In return for food, the children danced the *intore* or played traditional drums, but this Sunday Father had set up his projection screen in the gazebo.

Beni and I put down our butterfly nets and ran to take our seats.

I sat next to Mother on her bench, with Romeo at my feet. I turned to watch the workers saunter over and take their places. Beni, her *mama* and her *data* sat behind us quietly – she in her Sunday best and he reading from his leatherbound Bible. Beni played with the beads at the ends of her braids.

Sebazungu sat on the bench next to ours. Mother avoided his gaze. His wife, Mama Ruku, sat on a mat at his feet, their baby son tied to her back. Mama Ruku wasn't one of the wives who came to the back door for medicine on a Thursday; Mama Ruku had a job of her own selling bananas at the market in town. When Fabrice passed round the chicken and sweet potato Sebazungu ate his food before his wife ate hers. He then supped from a calabash of banana beer before offering any to her.

With everything ready, Father sat down and brought up the first slide. It was of a tall, good-looking man in a golden headdress like a lion's mane – the gardeners gasped at the giant black-and-white image on the screen.

"Some of them haven't seen photos this big before," explained Mother, though she didn't need to: I knew not everyone had a father with a projection screen, not even in England.

"Can you guess who it is?" Mother asked me.

From Father's stories I assumed it was one of the old kings.

"Rwabugiri," announced Father to the gathering, and a general murmur could be heard as the gardeners talked about the photo. It wasn't clear if they were discussing the dead king or the projected image that was to them quite real – as if the King might be alive again and standing in our garden. Several people gathered round the screen to touch the image; others examined the projection unit suspiciously.

Next came a picture of the villainous Queen Mother, Kanjogera, who looked nothing like the black-robed, toothless queen of my imagination. She was an odd-looking woman with a long oval face and droopy eyes. Glancing around I saw Fabrice tut and cast his eyes down.

Then Father showed a picture of King Musinga – the king who was naughty and wouldn't go to church. He had the same long face as his mother, but his eyes bulged and his receding hair was styled in such a way that gave the impression of horns. One woman found this image so disturbing that she screamed and only calmed down when her husband led her away.

After a while, when the cartridge needed changing, everyone got up to stretch their legs, sip banana beer through straws or reposition their babies. Mother went inside, Sebazungu went off to the yard and only returned when Father was showing pictures of the uprising. Sebazungu smiled broadly at the pictures. I thought it was odd that he should find images of burnt houses and slaughtered cattle so pleasing, but he wasn't alone: others at the gathering seemed to like them too. They lifted their beers in celebration. But not everyone was pleased. Celeste sucked her teeth, her large family sitting quietly beside her, their heads bowed. Her eye wept, and she rubbed her bad leg. It was hard to imagine that, if it hadn't been for Papa, Celeste would be dead.

And then came the image of Kayibanda, who Celeste had told me was Rwanda's first President after Independence. I thought he looked a bit like an American boxer. This photograph caused the biggest reaction of all. People got up, whooped and cheered and put on their coloured caps. Sebazungu supped his beer and said, "This was a good president."

At this point Joseph came running through the gate with a worried expression. Romeo cocked his head and lifted an ear.

"*Bwana, bwana*," he said to Father, trying to catch his breath. "Monty," he gasped, and pointed towards the flower fields.

"What is it, Joseph?"

Joseph motioned for Father to follow him, quickly.

"Come on, Arthur," said Father, turning off the projector. A groan of disappointment came from the crowd. "We'd better see what all this is about."

Father strode through the yard following Joseph, and I followed Father, taking two steps to his one. Romeo scattered the chickens. We walked past the cabbage patch, rhubarb and artichokes until we reached the cutting shed and the fields that stretched up into the mountains. Over the drainage ditch we went, and into the field of golden alstroemeria.

We crossed the field of spotted foxgloves – which reached to my waist and to Father's knees. As we broke out on the other side of the steep field we saw, a little farther on at the clearing where I was born, Simon and Thomas shouting at each other. Not just shouting:

fighting. Simon pushed Thomas, knocking off his cap, then Thomas pushed Simon, who fell to the ground.

"Stop," ordered Father.

Thomas backed off and Simon got up.

"What's going on?"

It was Joseph who pointed at the hut. Father went to it, and I followed with Romeo.

Monty lay gasping for breath on the floor. He was foaming at the mouth. Romeo sat down and guarded him. Monty's eyes looked like old scratched marbles and reflected no light. I stood in the entrance of the hut stock-still and watched Father press his head to Monty's heart. Anger seethed within me: I was convinced the witch was to blame.

"What happened here?" Father asked Simon.

Simon shrugged his square shoulders. Thomas looked at the ground. Father lifted Monty and pushed past them both.

* * *

"Blankets," said Father when we reached the house. I grabbed some from the pile in the corner and placed them on the floor for Monty, who lay like a heavy sack in Father's arms. Father laid him down and asked me to get Mother. I ran to her bedroom and dragged her by her hand through the house.

When Mother saw Monty almost lifeless on the floor, she knelt down and leant over him, covering him with her cardigan. Father moved aside and rubbed her back.

"There, there, Martha," he said.

"Can't you do something?" sobbed Mother. Her hair looked like tumbleweed, and tears poured down her face.

"There's nothing to be done. We just have to wait. It won't be long now."

Monty's breathing was laboured, but he looked to me as if he was fighting sleep, not dying.

Mother slumped beside Monty and stroked his brow. Tears fell from her eyes and onto Monty's face: it looked like he was crying too.

I wanted to tell Mother and Father about the witch. I wanted to say something so badly it felt as if my throat might burst. In the end all that came out were a few strained grunts that nobody understood but me.

* * *

Monty died just before sunset. By the time it was dark and everyone had gone home, Joseph had dug a grave in the front garden. He chose a spot next to Monty's favourite bush.

Mother, Fabrice, Joseph, Romeo and I stood over the dark hole, and Father knelt to lay Monty down. He was wrapped in his favourite blanket. Fabrice gave me a bone to bury beside him. I held my book; Mother held chrysanthemums.

Father said what a good dog he'd been, Mother sobbed quietly, and then, under the pale light of the moon, Joseph scattered soil over him, a gentle smattering at first and then great shovelfuls that thudded onto the tarpaulin.

As Joseph was filling the grave, an unfamiliar sound – a kind of pounding, came from up the road. I ran to the gate and saw a troop of about fifty soldiers, with boots and big guns, marching down the road. They passed the garden without looking in. I might well have dreamt it, had it not been for the fact I dropped my book in the mud, which left a permanent stain. Joseph picked it up, wiped it down and handed it to me. He gave me the thumbs up and led me back to the house before setting off on the first of his nightly rounds.

I sat on the front steps staring at Monty's grave. I thought about the soldiers and wondered where they were going and if they had anything to do with the changes the President was going to make. And I wondered how I could ever take my revenge on the witch for poisoning Monty.

Beyond the hydrangea bushes and the orange road, Nyiragongo glowed red in the moonlight. As I stood to go inside for the night, a gigantic boom sounded from the volcano, and the earth beneath me shook.

PART TWO

15

After Monty died Mother wept for days. Most of the time she stayed in her bedroom with a bottle of wine and the door locked, not even opening it for Dr Sadler, who visited each day bringing fresh fruit and chocolate. I kept out of her way for fear of upsetting her more.

When she was able to join us for dinner, Father told her that Monty had died from eating foxgloves. That didn't make sense. Why would Monty have suddenly started eating foxgloves – a flower he had never tried in his life? When dinner was over I took down one of Mother's botany books and looked up *Digitalis*, which I knew was the foxglove's Latin name.

I read all about how death by foxglove was extremely rare, and that a person or animal would have to eat a lot of it to die. It said that one of the first symptoms was sickness. If Monty had eaten the flower and been sick, he wouldn't have eaten any more. It was clear to me, if not to Mother and Father, that someone had intentionally poisoned him.

Mother's book said that another name for foxglove was witch's glove. I took this as a sign that the witch was definitely to blame – after all it was she who had snared Monty in the forest and she who knew how to poison fully grown men. But as time went by, I became less convinced by my theory. Monty had been found in the hut in the clearing, not in the forest; and Simon and Thomas had been fighting. There was something that didn't add up. I promised myself that somehow I'd find out what it was, since the adults were too concerned with the awakening of Nyiragongo and the arrival of the soldiers to care.

The volcano, Father told me, had suddenly awoken, like a grumpy giant who had been asleep for years. He said that when the giant woke he was so hungry his belly rumbled loud enough to make the earth shake beneath him. I knew it wasn't really a hungry giant that made the ground tremble, but Father's story was more comforting than the reality of a gigantic hole on the surface of the earth waiting to blow hot lava, ash and gas.

Over Christmas Nyiragongo resembled a huge red decoration in the sky. But when Mother took down the tree and the lights and the volcano still glowed, it became more sinister. It became a kind of warning light in the distance – but a warning for what I wasn't sure. I tried to ignore it, particularly before bedtime, when it glowed through my window like the red-eyed devil I'd heard about in church.

As for the soldiers, I had to try and piece together what was happening for myself, since nobody told me and I was unable to ask. About a week after they appeared, I heard

Mother say to Madame B. on our newly installed telephone that "soldiers living in Uganda had invaded from the north". I was meant to be studying in my bedroom, but the excitement made it impossible for me not to eavesdrop. Mother continued: "We're safe here on the plantation, particularly now that Belgium has sent in troops, but what about you? Are you being evacuated?"

After that conversation, Madame B. never came for coffee again. Neither did she hold another party nor shop for chocolate in town. And one day in November, when we were passing the tea plantation, we saw their high-security gates lying wide open and a dead peacock on the overgrown lawn. The sight of the peacock, dry and lifeless in the long grass, worried me more than the invading soldiers or the volcano.

"Don't worry," said Father when he noticed that I was looking back towards the carcass. "Things will settle."

"Why have the Belgian troops withdrawn so soon, after only a few weeks?" asked Mother. "Some of the gardeners are talking about Tutsis being beaten and left without food or water for days."

"Martha," said Father, laughing, "since when do you listen to the gardeners' gossip?"

I figured if Father was laughing there was nothing to worry about – neither the dead peacock on the lawn nor the Tutsis.

* * *

One Wednesday in January, Father tuned his radio to an English-speaking station that sounded very far away and unlike anything the gardeners listened to. He was in his study and I at his door when he caught me, but instead of being angry, he beckoned me in and sat me on his knee.

"Do you know about the Tutsis fleeing to Uganda?" he asked, ruffling my hair and spinning us round on his swivel chair. I nodded, remembering the story Celeste had told me. "Well, now the sons and grandsons of those people are coming back. They want to live in Rwanda: they believe it is their home." What he said made sense to me. The soldiers' families had been forced out of the country long ago. Why shouldn't they return?

Father went on to tell me about the invading army, the RPF, which had been trained by the Ugandans. They were strong and clever and spoke English, not French or Kinyarwanda. He said they wanted to "overthrow the government".

"But the government have told the people the soldiers are creatures from another world with pointed ears and tails – and the people believe them." The image of an army with pointed ears and tails was so strong that I almost believed it myself. "So now Rwanda needs soldiers to add to its army, which means we need to be careful not to let the government steal our gardeners." Father tickled me on the tummy, kissed my head and put me down. I thought about how the government might steal the gardeners. Did they have a butterfly net like mine, big enough to trap men?

I let out a little laugh at that idea and went to my bedroom to collect *African Butterflies* and my collection kit that I'd been given for Christmas.

In the garden, with Romeo at my side, I placed the kit on Mother's bench and set up the equipment on the table. When I had first received it I wasn't sure how I felt. Having spent three years gathering eggs, creating the perfect environment for them to hatch, grow and turn into butterflies, I felt uncomfortable about capturing and killing them. But *African Butterflies* had an entire section about collecting that referred to the "happy dispatch" of butterflies. It occurred to me that maybe death wasn't so dreadful – after all I'd watched Monty die, and that looked pretty much like he'd fallen asleep. I decided, after a lot of thought, that I'd give it a go.

The "killing agents" needed to put the butterflies to sleep weren't included in my kit, so Father had brought me a selection from the laboratory, and for the first few attempts he supervised me in the garden.

First we tried cyanide. I ran up and down the garden, jumping over rose bushes and tumbling into hydrangeas while chasing after a citrus swallowtail that looked like a black-and-yellow bird-of-paradise feather floating above me. After several failed attempts to catch it in the air, I crept up on it when it rested on an iris. I positioned the hoop of the net over the flower so that when the butterfly leapt up it flew straight into my net. Feeling very pleased with my catch, I ran straight to Father, who opened the bottle of cyanide.

"Cyanide's a good word, Arthur. Do you want to say it?" Increasingly I wanted to speak, so that I might talk to Beni, but trying to do it while poisoning butterflies was definitely not the right moment.

"Maybe another time," said Father, his tone dejected, as the fumes from the cyanide killed the butterfly. Watching it die didn't feel how I'd imagined it would, and it wasn't as exciting as the thrill of the chase. I thought I'd feel powerful, but mostly I felt guilt and regret. The butterfly would never fly again – and I was responsible. It felt terrible, and yet I couldn't stop staring, just as I stared at the wrecked trucks at the side of the road on the way to town. I couldn't get over how quickly it had died and its colour begun to fade. I was able to watch life drain out of its veins – able to see it take on the appearance of one of Fabrice's faded tea towels.

Father encouraged me to have a second go – this time with chloroform, which he said wouldn't fade the colours. For this method we needed one of the little boxes supplied in the kit. They had glass bottoms for inspection and holes in the lid for the droplets of poison. After waiting several minutes for a forest leopard – a long, thin-winged butterfly that looked just like its name suggested – to land on a bright-pink gerbera, I managed to net it and place it in the box. I added a drop of chloroform and covered the holes with my fingers until the butterfly was dead. It felt as though I'd taken a pillow and smothered someone in the night. I didn't like that.

On seeing my discomfort, Father decided that a bigger receptacle was needed, and so we tried a milk bottle with carbon tetrachloride. We poured some onto Mother's cotton-wool balls and placed them in a bottle. The grey-and-white butterfly I'd caught fluttered frantically, much to my displeasure. The specimen we used, a one-pip police-man, was a skipper, so its curved antennae and folded wings became caught in the wool. Its capture and death looked like torture.

Father said he had a plan to improve on this – "a solution that will combine all our efforts" – so off he went to the house in search of more equipment. He returned with a large pickling jar, blotting paper, brown paper and string.

In his absence I had caught a gold-banded forester, which was bright blue, black and gold, and placed it in a little box. Father put a half-teaspoon of ammonia into the pickling jar, placed several layers of blotting paper on the bottom and put the little box into the jar. He then covered it with thick brown paper and tied it tight with string. Very quickly the butterfly in the box appeared to sink into a deep slumber. Killing with ammonia was just as I had imagined killing butterflies would be. Its colours were still strong, I hadn't felt too involved and the butterfly hadn't struggled. The ammonia, though smelly, felt like the best option for the "happy dispatch" of butterflies.

That Wednesday, my equipment ready, I caught my second-favourite butterfly, a crimson-tip, which looks as if a young child has coloured the edges of its white forewings in red crayon and then outlined its entire body with a black pen.

I spent the best part of an hour chasing it through the plantation with Romeo, from the side garden through the yard to the vegetable patch, cutting shed and fields beyond. It wasn't until we were at the foxglove field and it stopped for a while that I managed to net it. It was thrilling to see the butterfly close up. I took it back to the side garden and set up the equipment. That done, Father came into the garden and stretched out on the bench asking if I'd like a story while I worked. I nodded and placed half a teaspoon of ammonia into my pickling jar.

He began by telling me how Rwanda was granted independence in 1962: "It happened so quickly that people didn't know what it meant." He was still at school in England, but his papa had written letters telling how government helicopters had flown over the countryside dropping leaflets that explained all about it.

"Papa sent me a copy of the leaflet. It said things like 'Tutsis and Hutus must unite' – 'No one is allowed to steal' – 'Everyone must work hard' – 'Tax must be paid' – 'Bride prices will remain'."

The idea of paying for a bride seemed funny. I wondered how much Beni's family would want if I asked her to marry me, and if Father would have enough money to pay. Once, when Mother and I saw a bride in a huge shiny white dress with her bridesmaids walking by the side of the road, she told me that most people paid for brides by giving goats or cows. We didn't have a cow to give. It filled me with worry and sadness that someone with lots of cows might want to marry Beni and then I'd have to let her go. I put some blotting paper in the bottom of the jar to absorb the ammonia. It seemed to suck up some of my sadness too.

"Anyway," Father continued, "the government was worried that the Tutsis in Uganda might come back and cause trouble if there were big celebrations in the streets. So on Independence Day people were told not to celebrate, but simply to stay home and hug one another." I was glad not to have been alive then – the thought of having to hug everybody made me short of breath.

"A few days later, Papa was told there were Tutsis from Uganda hiding in the forest, some of whom were captured by the gardeners behind the cutting shed. And then, not long after, armed Ugandan Tutsis were caught on the road to Kigali. They had hand grenades, machine guns, pistols, ammunition and whisky, and carried notebooks full of names of people to be killed – mostly Hutu politicians." I put a little box with the crimson-tip inside it into the pickling jar, covered the jar with brown paper, tied it shut and left the butterfly to die.

"And then," said Father, with an incredulous look on his face, "Belgian troops were withdrawn. For the first time in almost fifty years Rwanda was left without any Belgian control. Even the King decided to leave."

The wheels of a car crunching up the lane brought the story to an end, and I ran to see who it was. I was surprised to see it was Dr Sadler, who never came to visit on a Wednesday afternoon.

"Hello, Arthur," he said, mopping his brow with his red handkerchief. "Any words today? No? One day you will." He was puffing quite a bit. I led him to Father, who shook his hand.

"Edward, this is unexpected. Cup of tea?"

"I might need a drop of brandy in that," said Dr Sadler and muttered something about strength and fortitude, which was a word I didn't know.

Once inside, Father asked Fabrice to make tea and took Dr Sadler into the lounge.

"Arthur," said Father, "be a good boy and look after Dr Sadler while I tell Mother he's here." Father went to tell Mother, and I sat on the couch with Romeo.

"He's a fine-looking dog," said Dr Sadler. I kept one ear on what the doctor said and another listening for Father. "What sort of dog is he, Arthur, can you say?"

Fabrice brought in tea and biscuits and told the doctor that Romeo was a mongrel. I was thankful Fabrice answered for me: Dr Sadler sat back in his chair, drank his tea and looked like he was about to fall asleep, when Father came back.

"I'll try waking her again in a while," he said, and I knew that meant Mother must have been drinking again. He sat down and poured himself a tea, then handed me a biscuit. Father was very good at sharing biscuits.

"Just thought I should pop by and let you have the news," said Dr Sadler, brushing crumbs off his chest and onto the floor for Romeo to snaffle up.

He said things such as "Ruhengeri has been captured", "the border is closed" and "fighting has broken out in the mountains". And he told Father, "There's a curfew from dusk to dawn."

"I'd better call the lab, tell them I might not make it in," said Father, when a knock came at the front door. It was so loud it made the doctor jump. Father opened the door: it was the witch!

"L-laura," he stammered. I wanted to hide behind the sofa. Father bravely went outside and shut the door. The door was made of glass and opened straight into the living room, so it was easy to hear what they were saying.

"What are you doing here?" he asked in a hushed voice. I supposed he was trying not to wake Mother. I waited to hear the witch's reply, but Dr Sadler started puckering his lips and making little whistling noises while drumming his fingers on the arm of his chair.

"Well," said Dr Sadler helping himself to another biscuit, "Fabrice certainly does make an excellent biscuit and cup of tea. Time I got a Fabrice of my own." Dr Sadler was beginning to annoy me, his blathering prevented me from hearing what was being said outside. "Of course, I had someone once, someone to press my suits and make me supper, but—"

At that point the door swung open and the witch came into the living room.

"I don't think it's a good idea for you to…" Father didn't finish his sentence. Instead, he closed the door between the living room and the bedroom corridor.

I clung tightly to Romeo and tried not to look at the witch.

"Hello, Laura," said Dr Sadler, attempting to rise from his chair, but he only managed a tilt before sitting down again. "How are you?" The witch put down her huge backpack on the floor and bunched her unruly hair into a ponytail. She didn't look quite so frightening with her hair tied back, wearing jeans and hiking boots.

"They've no right to force me out of my home," she said angrily. "They're bullies. If they had any balls at all, they wouldn't target a single white woman. Who the hell is going to look after the gorillas while I'm gone – check the snares?" I hoped the soldiers had set her caged gorillas free. "Who's going to protect them from the poachers? They can't stop me from going back. They can't."

"Best not to fan the flames," said Dr Sadler. I wasn't sure what he meant.

The witch knelt down and emptied the contents of her backpack onto the floor as if she was planning to stay. Father paced by the front door, switching glances between her and the bedroom corridor.

"Did you say a curfew was in place?" Father asked Dr Sadler, looking at his watch.

"Dusk till dawn."

"Perhaps—"

Mother opened the living-room door. She was wearing trousers and a blouse, but I could see her nightie poking out where she hadn't tucked it in properly. She stood in the doorway staring at the witch. The witch didn't meet her eye.

"Martha—" said Father.

"What's *she* doing here?"

"Her camp's been taken over," Dr Sadler answered for Father.

Mother noticed the doctor for the first time.

"Edward," she said, her voice calmer. She pinched at her cheeks, fluffed her hair and smoothed down her blouse, but didn't tuck in the bit of nightie that showed. "Excuse us," Mother said to Dr Sadler. "Albert."

They went into the back lobby and closed the door. This time Dr Sadler didn't make annoying noises, and the witch sat quietly on the floor sorting her things – clothes, camp gear and notebooks. We could hear everything they were saying.

"I want her out of here. Do you understand? I don't want her anywhere near us. I can't believe you would do this."

"I didn't invite her, Martha. She just showed up. Her camp's been destroyed. We can't just throw her out."

"*We* won't be doing anything; *you'll* bloody well do it yourself!"

Mother came back into the living room, put her hand on Dr Sadler's shoulder and said, "Edward," before turning to me and saying, "Arthur, bed."

It wasn't anywhere near bedtime – we hadn't even had dinner – but Mother's tone made it clear I should do exactly as I was told. She paid no attention to the witch, just turned her back on her and led me to my room. Mother returned to her bedroom, and I sat on my window seat, my butterfly in its farm next to me, looking out over the garden as dusk began to fall.

After a while Father, the witch and Dr Sadler went out to his car. The doctor got in, and the witch put her pack on the back seat. She and Father stood having a conversation I couldn't hear. The witch was no longer angry: she looked a bit upset. Father placed his hands on her upper arms and kissed her lips.

It was as if, for a moment, my world had stopped.

When it started spinning again, I wanted to bang on the window and scream "No!" But I couldn't.

All I could do was watch Father kissing the witch.

16

For weeks after seeing Father kissing the witch I tried to make sense of what I'd seen. I came up with endless explanations. At first I convinced myself that the witch must have poisoned Father. When Father had gone out to talk to her, they had closed the door: anything could have happened. The witch could have offered Father a drink, or something to eat, or even injected him with some potion like the ones the gardeners talked about. Had she cast a spell on Father to make him fall in love with her and out of love with Mother?

The longer I thought about these things the more I became convinced that this wasn't the case. A nagging doubt, like a tiny mouse trapped inside me, scratched away day and night, trying to find its way out.

Father began to stay even longer at work, and when he was home for dinner Mother wouldn't sit at the table: she'd take her food, and a bottle of wine, and eat in her room. From the moment I saw Father kissing the witch, Mother pretty much stopped talking. If it hadn't been for Fabrice banging pans, the scritch-scratch of Celeste's broom and the sound of the radio, the house would have been silent. Mother's silence made me more aware of my own.

Mother couldn't have seen Father kissing the witch – her bedroom didn't overlook the front of the house – but clearly she knew something. I thought she must be mad at Father for letting the witch into the house, for putting us all in danger, but as time went by I figured it must be something more.

Mother's drinking didn't just affect Father: she made the house staff and gardeners work longer hours, but for no extra pay, and she banned me from playing outside for the whole of February and March. I wasn't even allowed to go out on my eleventh birthday – which made me pretty mad. She said it was because of the "threat of soldiers", but sometimes I thought it was really because she was worried that the witch would come back and cast the same spell on me. I thought Mother was afraid I'd love the witch instead of her.

On those days I spent most of my time staring out of the window at Nyiragongo or at my butterfly in its farm, and I desperately wanted to tell Mother how much I hated the witch for killing Monty and kissing Father. I wanted to tell her that I'd never allow the witch to cast a spell over me (though I did wonder if the witch had a spell to cure my fear of talking). But just as I was trapped inside, the words were trapped inside me.

After my birthday, my concerns about Father, Mother and the witch were replaced by events around the plantation. At night I'd lie awake and listen to the gunfire that dotted the hills. Mother said if I ever heard gunfire outside I should lie down on my tummy and place my hands on my head. Sebazungu told me that soldiers were stealing crops and goats from the *shambas* at night, and anyone who got in their way was being shot. My greatest fear was that they'd try and steal from Beni's family. I wanted to tell her to stay out of their way, let them have her crops and remember to lie flat on her tummy with her hands on her head. I lay awake at night worrying about that a lot.

Once – when I'd sneaked outside to look for clues to find out who killed Monty – I happened upon thousands of pale-yellow false-dotted borders flitting about the field of alstroemeria. As I was wondering if this was how the butterflies at the crater would look, a helicopter passed overhead. I liked its shape: it was like one of the black tadpoles in the frog pond in the side garden. I stood gazing up at it in its pool of pale-blue sky and listened to the whomping of the blades. The blast from the rotors made funny patterns in the fields, sweeping the flowers and my hair flat and forcing the butterflies onto the ground. The helicopter came so close that I could see the pilots' faces – and they could see mine too. I waved, but they didn't wave back, which made me feel foolish. On one of the doors was a sticker of the Rwandan flag and a French flag too – it was blue, white and red.

Suddenly the pilots spun the helicopter round and began spraying bullets over our fields. Instead of lying flat on my tummy and putting my hands on my head I just stood there.

"Arthur!" came a shout from behind me.

Thomas and Mother were running through the field of flowers. And Celeste, leaning on her *fimbo*, was trying to get to me too. Thomas hurled towards me, blazer flailing, and scooped me up. He turned right around and took me to Mother. I'd never known him move so fast. He took off his blazer and Celeste wrapped it round me. It smelt of tobacco.

"Arthur," said Mother.

"He is OK, Madame," said Celeste.

Mother took me from Thomas and held me tight. I couldn't remember the last time she'd done that. The trouble was it didn't feel nice: it felt like I might die from being squeezed too hard instead of being killed by bullets.

"You mustn't do that, Arthur," she said, once we were in the safety of the kitchen. She sat me on the table and fixed my T-shirt and hair, even though neither needed fixing. "Do you understand?"

I nodded.

"I know it's difficult being stuck inside, but it isn't safe out there. You have to understand." Mother stared at me. It was uncomfortable. I wanted to tell her I did understand. I wanted to tell her that just because I didn't talk didn't mean I was stupid. Being shot at by a passing helicopter was lesson enough: I didn't need Mother lecturing me too.

"Well," she said, taking a step back and tying her robe tight. "Perhaps I haven't been doing enough to keep you occupied. Perhaps I should drink a little less wine and spend more time with you. How does that sound?" It sounded like a good idea. Since the witch had kissed Father, Mother had been drinking even more wine than after Monty died. It was clear that Mother's drinking wasn't helping at all.

* * *

A few days later, Mother stopped drinking altogether, and not long after that she was up and about with her hair brushed and wearing clothes instead of nightwear. She organized a new timetable of lessons for me that could be held inside and did her best to ensure I wasn't bored and tempted to go out. It took a while for me to get used to the new routine, and my knuckles were red from rubbing, but in the end we both settled into a rhythm and life felt almost normal again.

One Wednesday afternoon, I was reading from Mother's encyclopedia at the dining table when she said to me: "Arthur, I have a surprise." Mother having a surprise was a surprise in itself. It was always Father who gave surprises.

She opened the door to the back lobby – and there, in the dim light, stood Beni. A smile broke across her thin face, which was as sweet to me as a crescent moon rising at dusk. Her almond eyes looked even bigger than usual.

I desperately wanted to shout "Beni" – but as always I was taken over by the feeling that should I talk my throat would seize up and I'd struggle to breathe.

"I thought you could do family trees – does that sound good?" asked Mother when Beni had sat down beside me. My whole body ached to hold her hand, but I couldn't pluck up the courage to do it. "Arthur, why don't you get your photo album? It might be nice to show Beni some of your relatives."

I went to my bedroom, where I took the photo album from under my bed, which left a perfect square of dust-free floor. I thought about showing Beni all the dead butterflies I'd been collecting and pressing in my book, next to the flower from her hair, but somehow that didn't feel right. So instead I picked up the butterfly farm, which contained only a crimson-tip egg – a yellow jelly-like egg I'd collected in January to make up for the one I'd killed with ammonia – and our butterfly, which, over the months we had all been held captive indoors, had begun to look frail.

"She is weak," said Beni when I handed her the farm.

I nodded.

Mother laid out paper and pens and opened the photo album, apparently indifferent to the plight of our butterfly.

"Let's start with you, Arthur."

Mother asked me to write my name at the bottom of the piece of paper. She then told me to draw a line upwards and showed me where to write her name and Father's, with a lower-case "m" between them to indicate their marriage. Then we did Mother's parents. I showed Beni my only photo of them – two solid-looking people in heavy glasses with thick coats and wooden-looking hair. I also wrote the name of Mother's brother, whom I only knew about through Christmas cards that usually arrived in March. The photos that came in the cards were always of him and his family wearing denim jeans, Mickey Mouse sweatshirts and grimacing smiles. His family looked odd to me, but I put them in the family tree the way Mother asked, and before long a little cobweb-like diagram took shape.

"And then how about you put in Father's parents?"

I turned to the picture of Papa, so that Beni could see his stiff white collar and shiny shoes. She traced her finger over his image. I wrote his name above Father's and then added "m" beside "Immaculée".

"Ah, but Papa and Immaculée divorced," said Mother. "So we need to strike through the 'm'."

I did as Mother said.

"Immaculée is a Rwandan name," said Beni.

"That's right," said Mother. "Arthur's grandmother was Rwandan. Show her a picture, Arthur."

I shrugged and shook my head.

"I'm sure there's one," Mother took the album from me and looked through every page. "Wait here," she said, and disappeared down the bedroom corridor saying, "I know there's one somewhere."

With Mother out of the room I was more aware of myself and of Beni. I wanted to tell her about my feeling of guilt over killing butterflies, the visit of the witch, the helicopter that had sprayed bullets over the flower fields – and how she should be careful at night and let the soldiers steal her crops and goats if they wished. I looked at the paper and pens, and it was then that it occurred to me that I could write notes to her. I was about to start writing when Mother returned, saying:

"Here it is." And she handed us a black-and-white photograph of a tall, pretty lady. I'd tried to imagine what Immaculée might have looked like all my life, but at that moment I didn't really care. I didn't care that she looked nothing like the laughing ladies with yellow eyes at the shops. I just wanted to write notes to Beni.

"She is Tutsi," said Beni, interested in the photograph.

"Yes."

"I am Tutsi," she said, and began to draw a diagram of her own. She drew a web just like mine, but next to the names she wrote a lower-case "h" or "t" for Hutu and Tutsi.

"Very good, Beni," said Mother, looking at Beni's tree, which read:

Sogokuru (h) "m" Nyogokuru (t)
Data (h/t) "m" Mama (t)
Beni (t)

I was plucking up the courage to write a note about the idea of there one day being a little "m" between Beni's name and mine when Fabrice came into the room. He told Beni her mama needed her at home. I wanted to shout "Stop" and tell everyone to leave us alone so we could "talk" at last. But before I could do anything, Beni took her family tree and said: "Bye, Arthur. See you soon."

With Beni gone I felt the way Romeo must have felt when Monty died – a lone dog without his pack mate.

"I speak with you?" Fabrice asked Mother, and they went into the back lobby to talk. I sat at the table and stared into the butterfly farm. As I stared at the lonely, listless butterfly, I heard Fabrice ask Mother for a loan.

"Because of war and drought," he said. "It is difficult. Très difficile."

Mother said she would think about it and told Fabrice to return to work.

* * *

That night, when Mother was asleep and the moon was high, Romeo scratched at my door, which I opened. He ran to the back of the house, and I let him out for a pee. Only the sound of heavy wind through the trees and Joseph's muffled radio broke the quiet of the night. That was until I heard a creaking noise coming from the chicken coop.

I stood at the back door straining my eyes and ears and tried to understand what it was. I was scared that a soldier might be stealing our eggs. My chest grew tight with worry.

The sound came again. *Creak*. I saw nothing. In the dark the yard existed only in a palette of grey. *Creak*, came the sound. *Creak*.

I held my breath and wrapped my arms around myself to stave off the cold and fear. Squinting harder, I saw a flash of colour on the ground – shiny and red – Fabrice's shoes!

I breathed out and relaxed my arms.

Fabrice must be tending the chickens, I told myself, feeling foolish that I'd thought it was something more. I clapped for Romeo, who dashed in, and banged the backdoor shut.

17

I woke the next morning, not to the sound of the cockerel, but to Fabrice clattering pans in the kitchen. I looked at my watch: it was quarter to seven. I had overslept. I hadn't heard Joseph whistling through the garden, or his boots slapping against his calves. The mysterious events of the previous night came back to me. Why had Fabrice been in the chicken coop at such a late hour?

I went to feed Romeo, who was sniffing round the back door, keen to get out. I opened it, and out he ran.

In the kitchen I ate my two small green bananas and two slices of toast, which tasted of charcoal and warm butter. Then I took my bath, dressed and joined Mother at the table, even though I'd already eaten. Fabrice brought her sausages and tomatoes.

"You've forgotten the egg," said Mother.

"Sawree, Madame. No eggs today. The chickens no lay."

I understood then that Fabrice had been checking on the chickens because something was wrong with them. I thought it very brave and kind of him to come away from home in the dark, with the threat of soldiers all around, just to check on the chickens so that Mother might have eggs for breakfast.

"Can I have money for eggs from market?" he asked. I could hear Romeo yapping in the yard.

Mother was looking for her purse when Sebazungu came into the living room without knocking. Fabrice returned to the kitchen.

"Sebazungu, what is it?" asked Mother sharply.

"Madame, it is no good," he said. "The chickens, they are dead."

"What?" Mother said, as if she didn't believe him.

"Come, Madame, you'll see."

Mother, Sebazungu and I went out to the coop. The chickens, headless and mangled, were sprawled about the place. Romeo was gnawing on one. The jackals must have killed them. There was something oddly compelling about the sight: it gave me the same feeling as when the butterflies had died – thrill and regret.

"The coop, it wasn't closed properly," said Sebazungu, showing Mother the lock. "It was not forced."

I realized immediately that Fabrice must have failed to close it properly in the dark. I felt bad for him. Mother stood quietly for a moment, looking at the dead chickens, then she said to me, "Arthur, get Fabrice."

I didn't want Fabrice to see the dead chickens he'd been caring for, but Mother gave me one of her looks that I knew meant "hurry up", so I went and got him from the kitchen.

"Eh, Madame," said Fabrice when he saw the chickens. "So sawree."

"Fabrice" – Mother was using the voice she used to talk to me when she was disappointed at something I'd done – "how could you tell me the chickens hadn't laid, but not tell me the chickens were all dead?"

"I'm sawree."

"Fabrice, tell me what happened."

Fabrice said nothing.

"You didn't check the coop this morning, did you? You didn't know the chickens were dead."

"No, Madame."

"Why not?"

Again, Fabrice said nothing.

After a while, when nobody had said anything and everyone was staring at the chickens, Mother began nodding her head. The expression of clarity on her face told me she'd found the answer to her question.

"You knew there were no eggs to be collected."

Fabrice looked at his shiny red shoes.

"You took the eggs and left the coop open, didn't you?"

Mother nodded some more, as if it all made sense – which it might have done to her, but it didn't to me. I didn't understand why she was accusing Fabrice of stealing the eggs. Didn't she know that he had been here in the night looking after the chickens? Words welled inside me – it felt as if they might burst out like hatching chicks.

"You needed money. Did you take the eggs to feed your family or to sell?"

Fabrice continued to say nothing. It was as though he'd forgotten how to speak. I wondered if he too was feeling the pain of words welling inside him.

"Get Joseph," said Mother to Sebazungu.

I looked at my watch: it was after eight o'clock. Joseph would be at home, sleeping.

"And Fabrice – tidy up this mess."

Fabrice had almost finished clearing the dead chickens by the time Sebazungu arrived with Joseph in the pickup.

"Joseph, what happened here?" asked Mother.

Poor Joseph looked as if the last thing in the world he wanted to do was say what had happened – but, not being one to disobey, he began to tell the story. Sebazungu translated for Mother. I wasn't sure if Mother trusted Sebazungu to translate any longer, but she had no choice.

"He says, Fabrice came in the night to take the eggs."

I didn't want to believe that Fabrice had stolen the eggs, but Sebazungu's translation was correct. I understood.

"He says Fabrice needed the money."

Fabrice held his head low like one of the pecking hens; Sebazungu stood with his chest out like our rooster used to do.

"He says something disturbed Fabrice. He didn't lock the coop."

I was the disturbance: I had let out Romeo and banged the door. I was responsible for the death of the chickens and Fabrice being in trouble. That felt terrible.

"Very well," said Mother. "Everyone return to work, and I will decide what to do."

Mother spent the morning weeding, deep in thought. I sat guiltily in the yard doing the sums she had given me, with Romeo at my feet. At lunchtime she came in and went to the kitchen, where I overheard her say to Fabrice:

"I can't have a thief working in my home. You know that. I must ask you to leave immediately."

I was stunned. Fabrice had been working on the plantation since Father was a boy. Mother couldn't ask him to leave. When she returned to the living room, I wanted to tell her that it was my fault the chickens were dead. Fabrice was simply trying to feed Beni. If Mother had given him the loan he'd asked for in the first place, then he wouldn't have had to take the eggs.

"Arthur, Fabrice has been very bad," she said.

I wanted to say "They're only eggs" to defend Fabrice, but Mother's mind was made up.

"Eggs," she said, "are the thin edge of the wedge."

I had no idea what that meant – nor did I care. Mother, as far as I was concerned, had gone too far. But she was about to go further.

"I don't want you mixing with Fabrice's family any more. Do you understand? No seeing Beni. Ever again."

Mother might as well have told me that I was never to eat again.

I went to my bedroom and slammed the door.

18

Listening to the rain clattering on the tin roof, I read in the local paper of children dying on Nyiragongo from *mazuku* – pockets of carbon monoxide. I didn't wash, do my lessons or play with Romeo. Mostly I sat on my bed and thought about Beni and how one day we might be able to release our butterfly at the crater. Mother would leave a tray of tinned meat and fruit outside my door and try to talk to me, but I'd eat almost nothing and refuse to listen. I wasn't interested in anything she had to say, and I certainly didn't want to see her.

Since Mother had banned me from seeing Beni, I'd developed a fever and a cough. I was exhausted, and one morning my stomach began to churn. I had to get to the bathroom but, determined not to leave my room until Mother had gone outside, I waited and waited until I heard the back door close.

I got to the toilet just in time. When I peed, hot liquid burned out of me, and my willy was covered in sores. Without thinking, I went straight outside to Mother, who was picking rhubarb.

"Arthur," she said, and I took her by the hand and led her to the house. She didn't resist.

"Oh my," she said when she looked down the loo. The bowl was splattered with greenish-brown poo, and the water was red with blood. I took down my shorts and showed her my sores.

"Good God!" she said. "Let's get you to bed." She pulled up my shorts and took me to my room, where she tucked me in.

"I'll call Dr Sadler," she said, and went to the living room.

An hour or so later Dr Sadler arrived. I was reading my book in bed, learning about "pinning" – a way of securing a dead butterfly to a board with a pin through its thorax. I thought I'd like to try it with the butterflies I'd killed, and so I made little notes in the margins.

"Martha, how are you?" he asked.

"I'm not great with sickness." Mother let out a high-pitched laugh. "But when I saw his... well you know... I thought it must be something serious."

"I'm sure he's fine."

They went into the bathroom, where Dr Sadler said, "I'll take a sample." Mother let out a noise that sounded as if she might be sick, then the toilet flushed.

"All in a day's work," said Dr Sadler, laughing, and they came into my room. "How's the patient? Any words today?"

I put down my book.

Dr Sadler placed his hand on my forehead, breaking our silent agreement of never touching.

"Looks like he's got a fever."

I coughed.

"And a cough. Have you had itchy feet, Arthur?"

I nodded: I'd been scratching them for days.

"And a bad stomach."

"Plus the other thing," said Mother, waving her hand at my crotch.

"Arthur, may I take a look?"

"I'll leave you boys to it," Mother said, and I took down my shorts.

"Uh-huh," said Dr Sadler, taking a look. "OK, you can pull them back up." He scribbled something on his pad of paper and asked: "What's the book?" I showed him the front cover.

"*African Butterflies*. Very nice." Dr Sadler tore the piece of paper from the pad and went to look at my butterfly farm on the window seat.

"It looks like you know a thing or two about butterflies." He was examining my butterfly and the crimson-tip chrysalis that hung from a single silk thread. It was the shape of a conical shell I'd seen by the lake.

"Maybe you'll be a lepidopterist when you grow up," he said. I didn't know what a lepidopterist was, but I decided I'd look it up in the dictionary once he had gone.

"You know, a hatching chrysalis reminds me of the night you were born."

I wondered how Dr Sadler knew anything about the night I was born: Mother had been alone. He took a seat on the corner of my bed.

"It was a wet night. I remember it as clearly as if it were yesterday."

I wanted to tell him he was wrong: it had been a bright, moon-filled night – Mother had told me.

"I was sitting on my veranda watching the rain pour off the roof when someone started banging on the big gates at the bottom of my garden. It was clear even before my nightwatchman was out of bed that someone was in trouble.

"I collected my bag, got in the car and switched the head-lights and the wipers on before the gates even opened. It was Simon: he was soaked to the skin. I realized immediately that your Mother must be in labour.

"'Doctor, doctor,' he said, and got in the car. 'Madame in trouble. Baby in trouble.'" Dr Sadler mimicking Simon's loud voice and poor English made me laugh: for a moment I forgot I didn't believe his story.

"We drove through the night in the rain up to the planta-tion. The road was full of mud and the tyres kept slipping. There were times when Simon had to get out and push and I thought we'd never get there.

"In the end we made it, but that was the easy bit. Next we had to find our way in the dark from the house to the edge of the forest through the fields, which were also full of mud.

"When we got to the clearing, your Mother was in a bad way. You were stuck – neither in nor out – a bit like a half-hatched butterfly in its chrysalis. Sebazungu was with her, doing everything he could to keep her calm, but after several hours up there alone even he was beginning to panic.

"Your Mother was delirious. She kept saying 'the elephants' – 'that witch'. In the end I had to give her some medicine to calm her down."

I wanted to stop Dr Sadler and tell him about the stampeding elephants – the elephants that Mother had been trying to warn off because the nightwatchmen had been drinking and not doing their job properly. I wanted to tell him that the elephants had fled because of Mother's screaming. And remind him about the witch who lived up on the mountain. But my fever had taken all my strength, and even trying to grunt my frustration proved too much.

"We managed to build a *tipoy*, a sort of stretcher, out of sacks and fallen branches, and we carried your mother down the hill and through the fields in the rain. By the time we got to the house, she was barely conscious. I was sure she was unable to give birth alone, so I had no choice but to risk the car journey back to town and on to the hospital in Goma." Dr Sadler paused, took in a deep breath and mopped his brow before going on.

"I can tell you, Arthur, I've never felt so alone as I did that night driving with your mother in the back seat, Sebazungu beside her and Simon next to me. I don't think any of us spoke the entire way. Maybe we thought if we all concentrated hard enough on getting through, the rain might disappear and your mum would be OK. But by the time we crossed the border and arrived at the hospital she was barely with us. I was convinced that neither of you would make it. But you came out fighting. Sadly your Mother took several weeks to improve."

I wanted to tell Dr Sadler that he was mistaken. But perhaps, I thought tentatively, there had been no elephants after all. Perhaps Mother had lied or imagined everything. And where had Father been during all of this?

"So there it is, Arthur, the story of your birth. I'm sure you've heard it all before, but it's not often I get a chance to talk about it." He got up and went to the door. "I had better give this prescription to your mum," he said, waving the little piece of paper. He went to the lounge, where I heard him say: "Looks like a good old-fashioned case of schistosomiasis."

"Schistosomiasis?" said Mother. It sounded like she'd been told I was going to die. I wondered if that was the case. Was my disease something deadly? Dr Sadler had forgotten to say.

19

Father came home that night and told me my disease wasn't deadly. He said that if I took my medicine, I'd be better within a week – and I was. But being better didn't stop me from being angry with Mother. When she asked me in the lounge how I was, I simply turned my back on her, took down the dictionary and searched for "lepidopterist". The definition I found felt as familiar as reading my own name.

Lepidopterist /lɛpɪˈdɒptərɪst/ n. a person who studies or collects butterflies and moths.

Over the next few months I read it over and over in my head, forming the words with my tongue: "A person who studies or collects butterflies and moths." That was me! I was already a lepidopterist. Dr Sadler had given me hope. One day I would leave Mother and the plantation and study butterflies wherever I chose. And maybe, I thought, closing the dictionary and putting it back on the shelf, just maybe, I'd take Beni with me.

One Friday in April, when I was imagining Beni and I living together, surrounded by brightly coloured butterflies,

Romeo sneaked into my bedroom. He cowered down on his haunches next to my butterfly farm and inched his muzzle forward. I looked into the farm, and there, in the corner, lay my beloved butterfly – dead.

A deep, long groan broke out of me. I dropped down and stared at its tiger-like stripes and leopard spots. Romeo nuzzled up against me. I groaned again: a mournful, animal cry. Romeo pawed the farm. I placed my hand around it, guarding it from him. He got up and skulked away.

I don't know how much time passed before I finally managed to scoop up the butterfly, but the sun was low and the birds were quiet. Its velvet wings gently tickled my palms, and I could see its hairs and veins in minute detail. I felt a terrible sense of guilt for not having managed to release it at the crater.

When I was certain no one was watching, particularly Mother, I took my butterfly to the garden and buried it next to Monty. I placed a buddleia flower on the mound of earth and shed my final tear.

Later that evening Mother, Father and I went to the hotel. Father told me a ceasefire had been agreed and we were going to celebrate with a "slap-up meal by the pool". I didn't feel much like celebrating. I could think only of my butterfly buried underground.

Mr Umuhoza showed us to our table, where I positioned my book so that as many people as possible might see it and think that I was a lepidopterist. At eleven years old I felt certain I could pass as a grown up. That was until Mother said: "Arthur, how many times do I have to tell you, not at the table?"

I turned to Father, but he simply shrugged and tried to catch the waiter's eye. Mother took my book and put it in her handbag, saying: "You can have it after dinner, but not before."

We were given plates by the waiter and pointed to the patio by the pool, where the buffet table was laden with every nice thing you could imagine. Seeing that table cheered me up a little.

There was a table for bread, cheese and cold meat, and one for starters, soups and salads. There was another one for potatoes – chipped, baked, mashed and roasted – and one for other vegetables. There were five different sorts of meat and fish dishes, and a chef who was barbecuing sausages, steaks and goat brochettes. But, best of all, there were two separate tables for puddings: cheesecake, triple-chocolate cake, pineapple mousse, ice cream in ten different flavours, coconut tart and fruit salad with fruits I'd never seen before. I didn't know where to start.

"Just take a little of what you fancy, Arthur," said Father. "You can always come back for more." I wanted to start with pudding, but, knowing better, I followed Father's example and began with some bread, cheese, meat and salad.

We sat down with our plates stacked high and looked out at the pool. The water was lit from below, and lights shone through the surrounding plants. It looked beautiful, even to a boy who had just lost his butterfly and didn't like to swim. We watched the ladies in their swimsuits lying on the loungers, talking to each other and giggling coyly at passing men.

I was about to go back for more food when a shout turned my attention to the bar. It was the witch again! Mother rolled her eyes and sighed. Father cleared his throat and concentrated on his food.

The witch was sitting by the corner of the bar, clutching a drink. Also at the bar was the lady with the pineapple hair, wearing only a bikini top and sarong and surrounded by men. Every time the witch shouted, the group of men grew smaller.

"Arthur, go and get something else to eat," said Mother.

At the buffet table I dolloped several spoonfuls of mashed potato onto my plate. Then a waiter behind hot urns lifted each in turn, so that I could decide which meat dish to have. I pointed to the lamb stew.

Returning to my seat I saw Mr Umuhoza and Sebazungu arguing by the pool. I couldn't imagine why Sebazungu would be at the hotel on his time off – it was a place only Europeans and Americans could afford to go to – or why he and the hotel manager should be fighting.

Tucking into my stew I watched Mr Umuhoza leave Sebazungu and approach the witch. He stood in such a way that he blocked her from the lady with the pineapple hair and the one remaining man. Whatever Mr Umuhoza said, it didn't appear to calm her down. The witch threw up her hands and slurred her words. After a while he gave up and came to ask Father for help.

"I'm sorry to ask," he said, and Mother put down her cutlery and gave Father a severe look.

"Why don't you phone Dr Sadler?" said Father to Mr Umuhoza. This seemed to please Mother a little.

"Certainly, sir," he said, and left the bar.

At that point a troupe of traditional dancers came in. They wore beads across their chests, wrap skirts, long grass wigs, held spears and had bells on their ankles. They began to dance in the centre of the room, in between our table and the bar. Through the thrusting heads and hair, brandished spears and arms held wide I saw Sebazungu go up to the witch. The drumming started, bells jangled, ladies ululated and spears pounded – all of which prevented us from hearing their conversation. Sebazungu stood, tall and strong, inches from the witch. His face was so close to hers it almost touched. He spoke quietly, his eyes fixed: he barely blinked. The witch, growing more and more irritated, tried to get out of his way. She moved from side to side and back in her stool, but he mirrored her moves. In the end she pushed him, jumped up and, just as the dancers and drummers paused for breath, shouted: "All poachers and pimps should be hung!"

Mother looked aghast. Father closed his eyes. I didn't know what a pimp was, but I knew about poachers and that the witch was one. I couldn't understand why she'd want to be hung. Before I could think of an answer, Dr Sadler arrived and led the witch away. They moved to the wicker seats. Sebazungu left the lounge.

After the fuss had died down, Mother handed me my book and gave me permission to have pudding. At the buffet I took the biggest bowl I could find and filled it up to the brim with every type of dessert. Then I went to the pool and sat down under the palm tree, where nobody could see me.

There I gorged myself until I was so full my sadness subsided and I couldn't manage another drop. I rubbed my belly and watched the ladies on the loungers, their breasts spilling out of their swimming costumes, then Sebazungu suddenly appeared with Beni. I was so thrilled to see her that I jumped up and started towards her. But as I got closer I saw that Beni didn't look the way she usually did. She looked thin; her eyes were small and her mouth tight. And she had make-up on.

Sebazungu had his hand on Beni's shoulder, but it looked as though he was steering her, not guiding her. He took her over to the lady with the pineapple hair, who had joined the other ladies on the loungers. She looked Beni up and down and turned her around, then held Beni's chin and moved her head from side to side, examining her face.

The woman nodded at Sebazungu, who held Beni close, kissed her forehead and touched her bum. She flinched. He then brushed his lips against her nose and lips and ran his hand over her small breasts, then rubbed her farther down, under the hem of her short skirt. Beni was stiff and tense, as if she wanted to resist but couldn't. Sebazungu stepped away and called to someone behind him. Out from the shadows of the trees came Sammy, who pulled Beni roughly away by the hand.

I was up and after them in an instant, through the bar and down the corridor towards the entrance foyer. I was aware of my grunting – anger and words trying to break out of me – but I didn't care. My gut told me I had to get Beni away from him.

"Arthur, where are you going?" said Mother, stopping me in my tracks as Sammy pulled Beni up the stairs to the bedrooms. I pointed in their direction.

"No, no," said Mother, ignoring my grunting and gesticulating. "We're going home. Come on, your father's waiting." She took me by the hand and led me away.

As I got into the car I was impelled, like never before, by a desire to talk, to tell my parents that Sammy had taken Beni upstairs, that we had to go after them. I grunted the words I fought to say, almost choking myself in the process. I even banged on the car window, but Mother and Father ignored me, just as they ignored each other.

By the time we arrived home I was so cross with my parents I couldn't bear to be under the same roof as them. Without thinking I picked up my torch, a bottle of soda, pulled on my jacket and went out back leaving Romeo behind. I hurried through the yard and took to the fields, where I stomped through Mother's flowers, deliberately damaging them, until I reached the clearing and the tunnel to the forest.

I didn't pause at the entrance – the soldiers had stopped fighting, the elephants didn't exist, the witch was at the hotel – the forest was hazard-free. I pushed on, farther from Mother and Father, through the trees and the gate, towards the top of Mount Visoke.

The fact that it was pitch-dark didn't bother me, nor did the fact that I was breaking the promise I'd made to Father not to go up the mountain, since he'd broken his part of the promise.

I scrambled up the steep ascent, which led to the witch's camp. When I arrived, I found it no longer looked the way it had before. The cabins were dilapidated; there were no Christmas lights and no socks or boots criss-crossing it. The bath was filled with empty bullet cases, the grass burnt out, and discarded bits of soldiers' kit were littered about the place.

Not wanting to hang around, I kept going up the path. My torch continually lit a circle of fern, moss and bamboo six feet in front of me. I felt nettles sting my ankles and vines tangle round my shoes, but I tore my feet away and pushed harder.

I was growing short of breath when I slipped on something wet. I managed to catch myself from falling and swung my torch to the ground. There, in the pool of light, was what looked like dung – not the elephant dung I might once have imagined it to be, but what I could only assume was gorilla spoor. Gorillas were the only mammals that could survive that far up the mountain and produce such a large amount of excrement. And the spoor was wet, which meant it was fresh. I knew the gorillas must be close.

Stopping for a drink I noticed hoops of wire – spring traps – all around my feet, which were covered by only a light layer of dirt. I used my bottle to test one. It was snatched away instantly and hung, swirling above my head, from the noose attached to a bamboo pole. Within seconds footsteps approached, a poacher let out a cry, a dog howled, and the din of the clappers on its collar rang out. I hid behind some bamboo and held my breath.

Somehow it didn't surprise me when Sebazungu appeared and checked the snare. On seeing the bottle dangling above him he swore and looked over his shoulders. As he untangled the bottle, the tip of his glove caught in the wire and tore. He tossed both gloves into a hollowed-out *hagenia* stump and left.

When I was sure he was gone, I flashed my torch in the stump. Inside it were bits of wire and string, a knife, two bottles of beer and a tobacco pipe. Maybe it was Sebazungu – and not the witch – who had snared Monty a few years ago, I thought, and a chill crept up my spine. Perhaps the witch didn't snare and cage gorillas, after all, perhaps Sebazungu did. Not wanting to dwell on the thought, I pushed on towards the crater, flashing my torch from side to side.

A little farther on, in a glade of brambles and thistles about thirty feet from the path, I happened upon a band of gorillas huddled in sleep. A baby suckled at her mother's breast. To one side sat the silverback, his fur bathed in moonlight that had crept out from behind a cloud. He woke and looked up. His smell was of sweat and manure. Our eyes met. "Agh-mmm," he grunted. My breathing all but stopped. He looked away, scratching himself uninterestedly.

I don't know how long I stood watching those creatures. It felt like seconds, but it may well have been hours. In the end I broke away and climbed higher. The farther I went, the colder it got. Mist and drizzle clung to me as if I was climbing into the clouds.

Then, just as I thought my lungs might burst, the mist lifted and I found myself at Visoke's summit. I could see for miles, all the way to Nyiragongo. It was exhilarating to be up there alone, free from Mother and Father. The crater was filled with a silver lake that shone in the dark. It must have been over a hundred metres wide. Scraggly evergreens stood round its edge like worn-out sentries.

I sat on the grass, which was dotted with clover and wildflowers, and stared at the reflections cast on the lake. A crescent shadow on one side, like an eyelid, gave it the appearance of the silverback's eye. It was almost perfectly still. The only sound I could hear was the throbbing of blood in my ears. I lay down and stared into the stars.

And then, when I'd been lying there for a while, a great rabble of tiny blue butterflies appeared. At first, it didn't look real – an indefinable mass of blue. They flew like confetti fluttering in the breeze. It was so quiet on top of the mountain I could hear the movement of their wings. A sudden rush of sadness hit me. This was where my butterfly belonged, here on the mountain, not buried under a hydrangea bush. I wished more than ever that Beni was with me, and that we'd set our butterfly free.

20

As dry season turned to wet, I struggled to grow used to the absence of Beni, whom Mother still forbade me to see. I wondered how she was, and spent much of my time alone in my room, feeling empty without her. I'd imagine holding her hand, and sometimes, early in the morning or late at night, I'd imagine kissing her too. When I thought about kissing her, things began to happen to me physically that I didn't want Mother to know about. If Father had been home I might have thought of a way of explaining to him, but he spent more and more time away, and we rarely saw each other.

Despite my loneliness, the ceasefire continued and my old routine gradually fell back into place. One Thursday I went out to Sebazungu's office to find him going through the filing cabinet. I saw his black-leather glove with one fingertip missing poking out through the files.

"Today you add up the hours," he said, slamming the drawer shut and throwing the sign-in sheets onto the table. The sheets that were used by the staff to log in and out each day. I lifted them grudgingly – the anger I had directed at the witch was now aimed at him. I could never forgive him for killing Monty or snaring gorillas.

Sebazungu left and I went through the sheets, trying to figure out the signatures and the thumbprints of those who couldn't write. I added up how many hours each member of staff had worked and multiplied this by their hourly pay. Sebazungu would then give everyone their pay on Friday. When I was almost finished, Joseph popped his head round the curtain.

"Sebazungu?" he said, and I pointed in the direction of the cutting shed.

He went off, his boots slapping against his calves, and returned a moment later with the key to the filing cabinet. With a screech from the drawer he took out a file. Sebazungu's fingertip-less glove fell to the bottom. Joseph locked the cabinet and left with a grin that exposed his gappy teeth. I finished my calculations, gave the totals to Sebazungu and went to my room, where I remained for the rest of the day, thinking about Beni.

That night, after dark, when the house was quiet, I heard footsteps outside and, not long after, the faint screech of the filing cabinet. I guessed it was Joseph doing his nightly rounds and putting back the file he'd removed earlier. But when I went to the kitchen for a glass of water and I looked out into the yard, I saw Joseph sound asleep in his lookout surrounded by empty beer bottles. Feeling tired I thought no more about it; I flung Romeo some scraps and went back to bed.

The next morning, when Mother didn't arrive for our English lesson, I went outside and found her talking to Sebazungu and Joseph, who was holding on to his pay packet.

"Oh Arthur, thank goodness. Let's have English class here today," said Mother with a wink that implied a game just between her and me. "Grab a pen and a piece of paper from the office and hurry back." I did as she asked and returned a moment later. "Sebazungu, I'd like Arthur to practise translation from Kinyarwanda to English. He'll write down whatever you and Joseph say." That wasn't something we usually did in English lessons, but it sounded like fun, so I went along with it. This is what they said:

JOSEPH: Madame, I have been given the wrong pay.
SEBAZUNGU: He is lying. He is trying to deceive you.

Joseph tried to respond, but Mother stopped him. She read what I had written and let out a weary sigh, then asked me to get the sign-in sheet for the week. She did the calculation in her head and took Joseph's pay packet, which she counted. "He's right: it is short," she said.

I wrote that down in Kinyarwanda and showed it to Joseph, who could read a little but couldn't write. Then they said:

SEBAZUNGU: Madame, that is because he has already spent it on beer.

JOSEPH: That is not true.

SEBAZUNGU: He is a thief. This morning there was money missing from the filing cabinet – and my leather gloves have also gone. He stole in the night. Who else could have done it? I'll bet his dirty prints are all over the drawer.

Joseph said nothing. I thought about writing that Joseph had been asleep when the filing cabinet had been opened in the night, but I didn't want him to get in trouble for sleeping on duty.

"Well, let's see, shall we?" said Mother, and we all went to the office to examine the filing cabinet.

There on the cabinet was Joseph's distinctive thumbprint from where he'd opened it the day before. I looked in the bottom of the drawer to prove that the gloves were there – but they weren't.

"Joseph," said Mother. "Go home. I will talk to you this evening."

With Joseph gone, Sebazungu explained to Mother that his stolen gloves had one fingertip missing – and if she saw anyone wearing them, could she tell him? I wondered who else had access to the filing cabinet other than Sebazungu, knowing he was the only one with a key. I went back to my room to think about Beni. After that, the day went along as normal, until just before dinner, when Celeste knocked on the living-room door. I couldn't remember Celeste ever interrupting before dinner.

"What is it, Celeste?" asked Father, who was home from work and reading his paper on the sofa.

"It is no good, *bwana*."

"What's no good?" said Father impatiently. I could tell he'd rather have Mother deal with the staff, but she was trying to make dinner, because she still hadn't found anyone to replace Fabrice.

"Ms Laney," said Celeste, and she looked at the floor.

"What's she done now?" Father put down his paper.

"Nothing, *bwana*." Celeste paused.

"Well?"

"Ms Laney, she is dead."

"What?"

Celeste did not repeat herself. She said only, "It is true," and continued to look at the ground.

"Where is she?" Father's face was the same colour as the grubs I used to find in the cabbage patch – a creamy white. He sat quite still for a moment, as if he was dead too.

"Visoke."

Father put on his coat and picked up a torch. I did the same.

"No, no, Arthur," he said. "You stay here with your mother." He zipped up his coat and went out the back door.

"Albert," said Mother from the kitchen when she heard Father leaving. "What's the matter?"

"Some trouble up the mountain," he answered. "Stay here and call for Dr Sadler."

Mother called Dr Sadler, and then we ate the plain pasta and salad she'd made, in front of the fire Celeste had prepared before she'd gone home. We watched the flames crackle and spit.

"I wonder what's going on," Mother said to the flames. I thought of writing "the witch is dead", but I guessed she wouldn't believe me, so I didn't. I doodled in the back of my book instead.

When the flames were growing shorter and the embers brighter, the sound of Dr Sadler's car broke the quiet. The beams from his headlights crossed the living-room ceiling as he pulled up outside.

"Everything OK?" he asked Mother when he entered.

"We're fine, Edward. Albert says there's trouble on the mountain. I don't know anything else."

It was then that the back door opened and Father came into the living room. Romeo jumped and sniffed around him as though he hadn't seen him in days, but Father ignored him.

"Everything all right, Albert?" asked Dr Sadler when Father sat down by the fire without saying a word, staring into the embers.

"Albert," said Mother, but Father shook his head.

"I'll make tea," said Dr Sadler, and he went to the kitchen.

Mother, Father and I sat in silence while he was gone. Father continued to stare into the fire, Mother squeezed her fingers, I tickled Romeo.

"Take some," said Dr Sadler, when he came back, pouring Father a steaming cup of tea. "You need something hot and sweet." Father hid his face in his palms and then rubbed them slowly down his face.

"She was just hanging there," he whispered.

"Who?" asked Mother.

"Laura," said Father.

Mother and Dr Sadler looked at each other as though Father had gone mad.

"She was hanging from a branch with a broken neck." Tears welled in Father's eyes. Mother sat on her chair as if she was glued to it.

"Laura's dead?" she asked.

Father nodded.

"Where is she?" asked Dr Sadler.

"In the cutting shed. Joseph and I carried her down."

"What happened?"

"She was gagged, tied up and hung. Probably poisoned too," said Father. I imagined the witch hanging like an antelope from a noose. "I found this glove in a stump close to the scene." Father produced Sebazungu's black-leather glove with one fingertip missing. My blood turned cold.

"Oh God," said Mother, and she held out a shaking hand. Father gave her the glove. "This is Sebazungu's. He tried to tell me this morning that Joseph had stolen it from the filing cabinet."

Why I didn't either write something down or attempt to say something at that point remains a mystery to me. I knew Joseph hadn't stolen Sebazungu's gloves. Joseph wasn't the killer. Sebazungu was.

Mother went out to the yard, where she dismissed Joseph immediately. Poor Joseph knew nothing of what she was saying. It was only after Father got up from the fire and went outside to translate that he knew he was being accused of theft and murder, and that he no longer had a job.

21

The next day Dr Sadler called Ms Laney's family in America from our phone to say she had died. He didn't mention the bit about her being gagged, tied up and hung. He told them she'd been drugged with digitalis – which, he said, "would have made her sleepy, so she wouldn't have felt a thing".

I was the only one who made the connection between Ms Laney's death and Monty's. Sebazungu had hung Ms Laney, after poisoning her with digitalis, and now I knew for certain that the witch hadn't killed Monty: Sebazungu had. I figured, that Sunday at the clearing, Simon must have been trying to hide Monty's body for Sebazungu and Thomas was trying to stop him. Nobody knew Sebazungu was a killer. It was the biggest secret of my life.

Dr Sadler told Father that Ms Laney's family had said, "She was happiest in Rwanda, and that's where she'd want to remain." Father received the news with a nod and took a swig of whisky from his glass. After a long discussion, they agreed that although Ms Laney's camp had been destroyed by soldiers, it was still the best place for her grave, close to the gorillas she loved so much.

Ms Laney was buried two days later. Very few people came to her funeral, on the plateau where wild primroses used to grow. Dr Sadler, Father, Mother and I stood together in the damp mist. Sebazungu stood on one side of the priest and Simon stood on the other, in his floppy hat (even though the sun wasn't shining) and blue dungarees. I couldn't understand how Sebazungu could stand by Ms Laney's grave looking sad after killing her with his own hands.

There was also a small group of men in camouflage gear by the graveside whom I didn't recognize. I thought they might be soldiers, but Father told me they were gorilla trackers who'd worked with Ms Laney. Being a gorilla tracker sounded like a great job: spending your day following the gorillas through the mountains must have been as exciting as studying butterflies. If I hadn't already decided on being a lepidopterist I might have decided to be a gorilla tracker instead.

We gathered round the hole where Ms Laney's body lay. Rain formed puddles in the tarpaulin that was wrapped around her body. The priest began to talk. He spoke so quickly in Kinyarwanda that it was hard to follow, but his voice sounded as if he didn't much care.

Once the priest had finished and we'd bowed our heads in prayer, Dr Sadler cleared his throat and said he'd like to add something. Over her grave he told the story of Ms Laney's life in Rwanda, of how she'd always battled for what was right – and not necessarily for what was popular – such as the end of poaching and Tutsi prostitution. When he spoke of those things he looked directly at Sebazungu, who stared straight through the doctor as though he wasn't even there.

Dr Sadler said he hoped the rumours and myths surrounding Ms Laney's life, such as her poisoning men and snaring and caging gorillas would go with her to her grave. At that point I looked away from the doctor and into the hole: I didn't want him to know I had been guilty of thinking those things about a dead lady.

"And now," said Dr Sadler, when he had finished his speech, "I invite Albert, an admirer and fellow researcher of Laura's, to draw the service to a close."

Father took a step forward, but Mother put out a hand to stop him. His face was so drawn you could make out the bones of his skull. He obeyed Mother, and instead of talking he simply laid a bouquet of flowers he had picked himself on top of Ms Laney.

I didn't know what to feel at the funeral. Looking into the hole, all I could think about was Beni and how much I wanted to be able to tell her that the witch had been killed and how, whatever Beni had been doing with Sebazungu at the hotel, she must not trust him any more.

When the funeral was over and Dr Sadler had left the house, having drunk several pots of tea and eaten almost an entire packet of biscuits, Mother sent me to bed. I lay in the dark, with only the glow from Nyiragongo to light my room, and thought of Beni. I heard my parents' voices coming from Mother's room. I knew the conversation must be important, as Father rarely went into her bedroom.

Father's voice wasn't loud and bright the way it usually was – instead it was soft and dull, as if someone had turned a switch off inside him.

"I only wanted to say a few words," he said.

"You would have said something you'd have regretted. Made it obvious that you and she were—"

"What?"

"You know 'what', Albert. I've been putting up with it for years. You sneaking off at every opportunity to be with her. I might have drunk too much in the past, but I'm not blind."

"Martha—"

"Don't give me explanations or apologies. I dealt with it years ago. There's no point in going through it again."

"I—"

"Since Arthur was born I haven't been a proper wife, we both know that. It would be foolish to think your needs weren't being taken care of elsewhere. I accept that. I just didn't want the staff to find out by you blurting something out over her grave."

I wondered what Mother meant by not being a proper wife since I was born. Was it my fault they didn't talk much to each other or that Mother had drunk a lot?

"God knows how much business she lost Sebazungu by ranting and raving about the prostitutes at the hotel, and everyone knows she dismantled his snares," continued Mother. "I just don't think it's wise that he should know you were involved with her, that's all."

"For Heaven's sake, why not?"

"Because I don't trust him any longer, Albert. Something's changed. I don't know what."

I wanted to run through and tell Mother all about Sebazungu killing Ms Laney and poaching gorillas, but before I had the chance Father said finally: "You think I'm in danger from Sebazungu."

"I don't know what to think – and that's the point."

He said no more and went to his room.

I lay in the dark, not thinking about Beni but of Father instead. Mother was worried that Father was in danger from a murderer. That knowledge, that responsibility pinned me to my bed like a butterfly with a pin through its thorax. For once I wasn't fighting the words I wanted to say, for once the words didn't well within me or suffocate me. For once I had no words inside me at all.

22

1992

"Your Father hasn't told you one of his stories in a while," said Mother, trying to start the pickup – which eventually spluttered to life. We were going on a drive "to get out of the house and feel the wind in our hair".

We headed up the track by Beni's house. It had been such a long time since I'd seen Beni I wasn't sure I'd recognize her any more. I wondered if she had grown like me. I was almost as tall as Mother.

"Has Father told you about Kayibanda, the President of Rwanda after Independence?" she asked, driving out of the plantation, honking at people ambling along to get out of her way. I shook my head. All I knew about Kayibanda was from Celeste and the photo Father had shown on his projector.

"Kayibanda was a quiet man," said Mother, dodging potholes. "He rarely left his palace, but because he was the President, people obeyed him just the same, whether they saw him or not."

We bounced up the track – the pickup's exhaust pipe clattered on every stone, and it spewed out black fumes.

"Under the President, Rwanda was a lawful place: prostitution was punished, everyone worked hard and went to church on Sundays, just like they were told to do.

"But with time the President became more and more reclusive and spoke to his government less and less. His politicians began to squabble" – Mother tried to change gear, but the gearstick wouldn't shift and she had to fight it into position – "and one man in particular was keen to make the most of his weakness. That man was Major General Habyarimana."

I'd heard of Habyarimana: he'd been the President of Rwanda all my life. There were pictures of him wherever you went.

"He was a big man and a strong leader, and he decided he wanted to be President. Soon many of the President's men were found dead and their families paid to keep quiet.

"I'm afraid the story has a sad ending, Arthur," said Mother glancing over at me. The forest came into view. "After Habyarimana became President, there were rumours that Kayibanda and his wife had been imprisoned. People said they were starved to death." I thought that sounded horrid, and felt bad for the old president and his wife. "No one really knows what happened to the reclusive President in the palace. And, as you know, Habyarimana is still our President, but" – and she added this under her breath after we'd stopped and got out – "who knows for how much longer."

I wondered why Mother thought the President might not stay in power for much longer. The ceasefire hadn't lasted long, but around the plantation the gardeners were talking about peace, new ministers and a renewed ceasefire. Did Mother know something they did not?

"Fancy having a go?" she asked, holding the driver's door open. She moved the wheel from side to side and pointed at the pedals – which I understood to mean really having a go, proper driving, not just sitting on Father's lap and turning the wheel. I got in.

Sitting with the wheel in front of me felt a bit like getting on my bike for the first time. It was risky and strange, but exciting too.

"So, first things first," said Mother getting in the other side. "Before we start, we need to check the vehicle's in neutral." I wiggled the gearstick from side to side. "Good, now put down the clutch and turn the key." I did as she said, and initially the engine coughed, but then it roared to life. "Now move the gearstick into first – that's it – and push the accelerator as you release the clutch."

And we were off. I couldn't believe it. I was driving!

"Great, Arthur," said Mother. "This is fun!"

Little by little I became confident and learnt to change gears and go faster, under Mother's watchful eye.

"Best to slow a bit here," she said when we hit a difficult patch. She reached out to steady the wheel. I took my foot off the gas, hit the brake harder than intended and we rocked to a sudden halt. The engine cut out.

"You OK?" she asked as the dust settled around us. I nodded. "Well, let's just turn it back on."

Cautiously I turned the key, but nothing happened.

"Try again."

Nothing.

"Let me have a look."

Mother couldn't get it started either.

"It's not your fault," she muttered, getting out and lifting the bonnet. "This old thing's been on its way out for years."

As Mother tinkered under the hood, I sat by the roadside, worrying that dusk was not far away. It was dangerous to be stuck on the track after dark – gunfire rattled around the terraced hills most nights. Soldiers continued to raid the *shambas*, killing anyone who got in their way. I thought that if we remained on the road the soldiers might shoot us.

Mother was rubbing her brow with oily hands and making more and more noises of concern and frustration when a sound from the forest caught our attention. It sounded like the cry of a snared duiker.

"We should take a look," she said, closing the hood and wiping her hands on her trousers. "There's nothing more I can do here anyway."

I grabbed the torch from the glove compartment, and Mother reached for her pistol.

"Just in case it's in a bad way," she said.

I'd never seen Mother shoot anything before; I wasn't sure if the idea filled me with excitement or dread.

We crept into the forest, following the sound. I led, and Mother walked behind. I flashed the torch from side to side looking for signs of snares. Worried that Sebazungu might be checking them, I was glad that Mother had her gun.

Over the months since Ms Laney's death I'd done my best to keep out of Sebazungu's way. I even managed to get out of working with him on Thursdays by teaching myself to cook, something that Mother valued, given that we still had no cook. I couldn't tell if Sebazungu was aware that I knew he was a poacher and Ms Laney's killer. I pretended not to know. Sometimes that helped me forget my fear, and at other times – such as now, as I advanced through the forest with Mother – it filled me with terror.

Mother and I crept in deeper, until we came to a small dell where a group of men were gathered round a body on the ground. It shocked me to see the priest restraining Sammy, whose face was swollen – black and blue. Zach stood to the side of the dell watching Sebazungu, who was kneeling over the body. Simon had a hand in the pocket of his dungarees, rubbing himself.

Sebazungu flipped the body over as if it were one of the rag dolls sold for tourists. It was then I realized this was no rag doll – it was Beni, who was screaming herself hoarse.

The priest pulled Sammy's hair so tight he couldn't look away and said, "This is what the Tutsi deserve. This is what you should have done – broken her like a mule." Zach whooped in agreement.

Sebazungu undid the zip of his trousers and pulled at Beni's pants.

The priest, Simon and Zach looked on as if they were watching a game of football or some other form of entertainment. Sammy closed his eyes and fought to turn away.

"Jesus," said Mother when she saw what they were doing. "Arthur, stay where you are."

She stalked up to the men and put her pistol to Sebazungu's temple, saying that nobody should move.

Beni slithered on her belly away from him, into the long grass. I knelt down beside her and, without thinking, held her hand in mine. She sobbed heavily, unable to talk. I felt like crying too, but no tears came.

Mother pointed her gun at Simon, who knelt and begged not to be shot. With Sebazungu and Simon down, she motioned with her gun for the priest to let go of Sammy. He did so and joined the others on the ground. Zach quickly followed.

When the men were on the floor, Mother whispered something to Sammy, who ran off the way we had come. He returned with a rope from the back of the pickup. Together, Mother and he tied up Sebazungu, Simon, Zach and the priest, before rounding up Beni and me and guiding us home.

* * *

Mother never spoke to me about what happened in the forest, but I overheard her telling Father:

"We have to report them."

"There's no point – nothing will be done."

"Why ever not?" she asked

"Because they'll turn a blind eye."

I knew neither who "they" were nor who eventually freed the four men, but Sebazungu and Simon never returned to work, and we, as a family, never went back to church. With Sebazungu off the plantation I was no longer quite so worried about him being a threat to Father, and Sammy didn't frighten me in quite the same way either. On the walk back from the forest that night, it was clear that he'd been badly scared. As we walked Beni explained that her *sogokuru* had been forced to put her "to work" to feed the family. Sammy hung his head. Mother's face crumbled. I wondered what she meant.

For nights on end I thought about what those men had been doing, how long they had remained in the forest with their hands behind their backs and how Beni was feeling. I longed to see her again.

In time everything regained an air of normality. Fabrice was given his job back, and so too was Joseph. The fighting stopped for a whole dry season and the following wet one. The guns remained silent, and people went about their lives, tending their crops and animals. But best of all, I was allowed to see Beni again. The sense of emptiness I had felt without her all but disappeared.

Though it took her a while to recover from her experience in the forest, we spent most of our time together holding hands. And even though we had grown taller and Beni had grown fuller and begun to wear T-shirts and wraps instead of dresses, we still chased butterflies in the garden. One of the best days we shared was when we caught a second *Charaxes acræoides*, which was almost identical to the one now buried beside Monty. Father said that having had one was rare but to have had two was "something else". Then and there I hatched a plan to take Beni up to the summit where we could release this butterfly – just as I should have done with the first.

When we weren't catching butterflies we played Jenga in the yard. We spent hours sitting at the table we'd made out of a cooking-oil drum and a piece of scrap metal that Joseph had helped to hammer flat. Mother had bought the game from the wood-carving beggar in town – her one and only purchase from him.

One afternoon in August, when we were playing in the yard and listening to the radio with Fabrice, Beni whispered:

"It is the President on the radio." She removed her first block from the tower and placed it on the top.

She was right. The President was giving a speech that was being broadcast live to the nation. Fabrice

listened intently at the back door, absent-mindedly peeling potatoes; some of the peelings missed the bucket
and landed on the ground.

I concentrated on the game, carefully sliding out a piece in
the middle and putting it up top. The President was talking
about the importance of peace.

Celeste was in the yard too, sweeping. The scritch-scratch
of her broom made it difficult for Fabrice to hear, so he
turned up the radio. But Celeste went on sweeping, louder
and louder. Beni was taking her next block when Fabrice
shouted at Celeste:

"Be quiet!"

Celeste didn't stop.

Angry, Fabrice abandoned the potatoes, took the radio
and went inside. His shouting caused Beni to tremble: the
tower leant to one side but remained intact.

"*Sogokuru* is worried," said Beni anxiously. "Mama
say so."

I took a piece near the bottom and positioned it on
top.

"Everyone at home is shouting. *Data* say there is trouble
ahead." Beni looked concerned. I wondered if I should be
too.

When the President had finished his speech, Fabrice turned
off the radio. Celeste went inside and tuned it to another
station. She began ironing Father's shirts, leaving the back
door open.

"These people say President does not want peace," said Beni as she nudged one block but chose another, finding it harder with every move.

From where I was sitting I could see Celeste nodding her head at what the radio presenters were saying. When it was my turn, I inched out a piece from the tower, which began to wobble precariously.

Fabrice shouted from the kitchen:

"Turn the radio off!"

Celeste turned it up.

Fabrice threw a pan on the floor, which made Beni and me jump and the tower crash to the ground.

* * *

As the months went by, despite their differences, Fabrice and Celeste still took care of the house, leaving Mother, without Sebazungu, in sole charge of the plantation. More and more of the gardeners decided to leave, which made Mother unhappy. One night, over dinner, she said to Father: "I don't know what I'm doing wrong. They just don't obey me any more. I have hardly any staff left."

"It's not your fault," Father told her, clutching a tumbler of whisky. "Anyone and everyone are being recruited for training at the moment. God knows what's been planned behind closed doors."

I brushed my bare feet on the antelope skin and thought, "Training for what?" But Father switched subjects.

"I've been reading that children who grow up in multi-lingual environments often have delayed speech."

"Oh please," replied Mother, and cast him a withering look.

"It might be worth looking into, Martha. Maybe England isn't such a bad idea, given all that's happening here."

There was something about Father's tone and remote expression that made me feel uncomfortable. It must have shown on my face, because the next thing he said was:

"No reason to worry, Arthur. *You'll* be fine."

Why was I the only one who was going to be fine? I wanted to ask. Was I going to England? And what about Mother and Father and everyone else – were they going too?

Just as I was thinking this, Fabrice rushed into the room.

"*Eh, bwana*, you hear the radio?" he asked.

"No," replied Father.

"So sawree, *bwana*. Ceasefire over. War starts again."

23

Within weeks, most of the remaining gardeners were gone, leaving Mother to manage almost single-handedly a plantation that had once been tended by over a hundred workers. The fields quickly became full of weeds and dead flowers. The cargo planes that carried food supplies above the plantation would have seen nothing of the once perfectly ordered rows of flowers Mother was so proud of. Even her garden began to wilt and die. Her favourite roses turned from a brilliant, crisp yellow to a dull, soggy brown. The hydrangeas grew bushy and the grass long.

When the gardeners stopped coming to work, their wives did too, which meant Mother had to find new ways of transporting the few flowers she rescued from the fields. Sales dwindled to almost nothing, and although she said her income wasn't vital, I could tell she resented the war preventing her from earning money of her own.

"Come on, Arthur, we're going to town," she said one Tuesday in late February. We hadn't been to town since before Christmas, so I was surprised, though not disappointed to hear that we were going. I was fed up of sitting round the house waiting for the fighting to end.

The pickup was by the cutting shed, with flowers in the back that Mother had picked by herself. It wasn't full the way it used to be, and the flowers weren't as fresh or as brightly coloured either, but they still looked pretty.

"Run and get Thomas," she said, Thomas being one of the few remaining gardeners who still came to work when he could.

I found him, tall and even thinner than usual, in the field behind the cutting shed. He was weeding. Like the flowers, he had a withered, unhealthy look about him.

"Hello, Arthur," he said.

I pointed to the pickup and motioned for him to follow.

"*Oya*," he said quietly: he would not come.

Returning to Mother I shook my head, clapped for Romeo, and the two of us got in. But as Mother started the engine, Fabrice came out from the yard, waving his arms in the air and shouting.

"Whatever now?" said Mother, turning off the engine and opening the door.

"Madame," he said. "Where you go?"

"To town."

"Eh, Madame. No. The road is dangerous."

"The road is fine. Now get back to work. Arthur and I will be back for dinner."

"Madame—"

Mother turned on the ignition and revved the engine. It had been repaired, so the gears no longer crunched and the exhaust no longer scraped. The smell of smoke and manure through the dashboard had disappeared.

As we drove out of the plantation, I looked back in the side mirror to see Thomas chewing worriedly on his tobacco, Fabrice tutting and Celeste sucking her teeth and shaking her head.

Mother didn't drive quite as quickly as she used to. It was a cloudy day, and the track was more murky brown than orange; the lush green countryside was now the colour of straw. The drab reds and pinks of the flowers in the back streaked past the burnt-out landscape. It seemed that when I hadn't been looking the colours of Rwanda had changed.

The road was even worse than usual – the wet season and trucks full of soldiers had created even bigger potholes. I wondered why no one had thought to fill them in the way they used to. Where were the men with their shovels and hands stretched out?

"Hold on tight, boy," called Mother as we hit the narrowest section of the road on a tight bend, with a huge pothole in the middle. But Mother didn't call, "Here comes the fun!" – instead Mother swore under her breath and fought with the steering wheel. The pickup was at such an angle that two of the buckets fell out the back, scattering flowers on the road like at a funeral procession. The buckets tumbled down the steep bank and out of sight.

There were no women to look back on with enormous bundles of wood on their heads and babies on their backs.

There was hardly anyone to be seen anywhere except the odd tired-looking farmer standing by the roadside with a spear or bow and arrow.

The steep road to Gisenyi was much quieter than normal too. Instead of the huge lorries that swayed from side to side there were newer ones with white circles and red crosses on them that shed grain onto the tarmac. There were no *boda-bodas* laden with families and goats, no *matatus* bursting with passengers.

At the side of the road, where the prisoners in orange uniforms used to plough, there were now rows and rows of tents – small towns erected out of blue tarpaulin. The eucalyptus trees had been stripped bare for firewood, and the small children we passed had heads so big they resembled the lollipops Mother used to buy me at the shop in town.

Halfway to Gisenyi we saw men with spears standing in the road. They had made a barricade out of two oil drums and a long tree branch.

"What now?" sighed Mother, slowing the car to a halt and winding down her window. "What is it?" she asked the approaching man who pointed his spear into the pickup. He didn't look like someone who wanted to do us harm. He looked like one of the farmers we'd passed on the track.

"*Pasiporo*," he said.

Mother rummaged in her handbag, then gave up with a shrug, saying: "I haven't got it."

The man had a good look at me, and then at the flowers in the back. I wasn't sure what he was looking for. I wasn't sure he knew either.

Mother pulled out a chequebook and waved it out the window.

"Here," she said, and thrust it in his hand. When she saw him trying to read it upside down she rolled her eyes and let out an exasperated sigh. But the chequebook seemed to please the man, who gave it back to Mother and nodded to the others that they could let us through. They lifted the branch and Mother put her foot down, irritated by the whole affair.

We descended into Gisenyi, where we wound round the lake to the border with Zaire. The schoolchildren in their khaki shorts weren't there: soldiers in scruffy khaki uniforms had replaced them. Under these uniforms the soldiers wore bright T-shirts and hats that were falling to pieces. Some of them didn't look much older than me.

The foam-mattress shops were closed, and the decaying buildings in every colour of ice cream looked worse than ever. Crowds of people trudged towards the border. The petrol station had a sign up that read "*Pas d'huile*" and swung with a squeak in the breeze.

On our way to the post office we saw Madame Dubois with two suitcases getting into the back of a truck with lots of other white people. I wanted to ask where she was going and who was going to look after her topiary hedge. I knew things must be pretty bad if Madame Dubois was leaving.

At the post office Mother didn't attempt to negotiate the storm drain: it was clear that it was closed – the doors were shut and the windows boarded up. The shop for Americans and Europeans was shut too – which I thought would make Mother angry, but she just kept driving, taking in the closed-up town with all the people passing through, Nyiragongo looming above them.

The market was deserted: no haggling, big-bosomed women or bleating goats. The *boda-boda* drivers were nowhere to be seen. On a street corner I saw Sebazungu talking to a policeman. He saw the pickup and Mother saw him, but it was as if they were invisible to each other. Even the hotel car park, usually full of 4x4s, was empty.

"Give me a hand with the buckets, Arthur," said Mother after she'd parked. The beggar with his wood carvings wasn't there that day. As we lifted the buckets out of the back of the pickup, Mr Umuhoza came out of the hotel.

"Madame," he said. "I'm sorry. No flowers today. We have no guests."

Mother let out a deep sigh, and I put the buckets back in the truck.

"Do you still have coffee?"

"That we have," said Mr Umuhoza laughing, and he led us to the lounge.

Dr Sadler was the only other person around. There were no men in safari jackets, no big-bottomed women in shorts and long socks – not even the lady with the pineapple hair. Dr Sadler looked even more crumpled than usual.

"Hello, Martha," he said wearily.

"Edward," Mother said, then pressed her cheek against his and sat down opposite him. Coffee was served.

"And hello, Arthur." Dr Sadler gave a wan smile. He didn't ask me if I had any words that day. I sat next to Mother. "How are you both?"

"We're fine."

Dr Sadler raised an eyebrow.

"You do realize this is only going to get worse, don't you?" Mother sipped her coffee. "They're saying more than half a million people have already fled the country, with thousands buried in mass graves."

"Do you believe it?" Mother asked.

"Just look around. No food or fuel. Those who aren't dead already will be soon, if the conditions of those camps is anything to go by. You should get out while you can."

"Oh, don't you start," said Mother. "Albert's been on about that for months. He's decided we should go back to England and have Arthur grow up surrounded only by English speakers – he thinks it will help him to talk."

"I suspect that's unlikely."

"I agree, and besides, we're not leaving. I'm not just going to abandon all we've worked so hard for."

I didn't want to hear any more about Father wanting to send me to school in England. I couldn't understand why he'd suddenly want to send me to the place that had made him so unhappy as a boy.

"You may not have a choice, Martha. Some of the French and Americans have been rounded up already."

"Well, that's typical of the French," said Mother. "We're staying put. The fighting is mostly in the towns. There won't be any bother at the plantation, I'm certain of that."

Dr Sadler raised his shoulders.

"If what I hear is true, it may not be long until the RPF storm Kigali. Which means the government will soon be gone and anarchy will rule. Who knows what might happen."

"Nonsense," said Mother, still sipping her coffee. Obviously Mother knew what anarchy meant, unlike me.

"The people are angry, Martha, and one doesn't have to look too far back in history to see just what can happen in this country when the people decide to take matters into their own hands." I thought about Celeste's story of men killing one another with machetes and bows and arrows. Was the same about to happen again?

24

Nothing improved over the next six months. Planes carrying emergency rations flew over the plantation more frequently, and the blue tarpaulin camps grew bigger and bigger. Dr Sadler, who visited only from time to time, said that almost a million people had fled the country.

Fabrice told Mother stories of fighting and killings in the hillsides: it seemed the troubles were no longer confined to town. But still she believed we were safe. I doubted whether Mother was right. There were days when Celeste was too frightened to come to work, but Mother carried on as though nothing was wrong.

One evening I went to Father's study and tuned the radio to the station they'd banned me from listening to. Father called it the "Vampire Radio". Sitting in the dark I leant back in his chair and listened to the young, cool hosts broadcasting from Kigali. The African rock music they played was raucous and loud, but I didn't care. They told rude jokes about Tutsis, casually calling them "cockroaches".

"No one should think twice about stamping them to death and watching their guts ooze out. Tutsis have always been evil," they said. I thought about Beni and hoped she wasn't listening. "We the Hutus are innocent."

When the lights of Father's car came up the drive, I switched the radio off: he would be angry if he caught me listening to the Hutu station – and I didn't want that.

At the dinner table he said to Mother: "Have you thought any more about…" but instead of finishing his sentence he lowered his chin a little, raised his eyebrows and glanced between Mother and me. I knew he was discreetly trying to ask Mother about England.

"Edward doesn't see the merit in it," said Mother with tight lips and a slight shake of her head that meant: "This isn't the time to discuss it."

I was annoyed. Why didn't I have a say in the matter? Like so many other things that were happening, it didn't make sense.

It was hard to sit through the rest of the dinner. Mother ate with a vacant stare, and Father, who looked exhausted, kept letting out deep sighs. He told us that peace had been agreed and that the war would come to an end. He didn't sound pleased, nor did Mother.

"Maybe life will get back to normal around here," she said, unconvinced.

"We'll see," said Father, pushing his half-eaten plate of dry rice and beans away.

When Fabrice collected the plates, Father told him about the peace agreement, and Fabrice bowed his head and said: "Thank you, *bwana*. Now God may sleep in Rwanda again."

The candle on the table flickered out, and a moment later burned to life again. That flame was the final flicker of light I would know in Rwanda. Fabrice's hope of peace was about to be extinguished for ever.

* * *

In November, soldiers in blue helmets arrived. They walked around town with their guns slung low. Father told me they were there to make sure the fighting stopped, but not to fight themselves. They looked different from the other soldiers. Their uniforms were smart: blue neckerchiefs, polished boots, ironed T-shirts and trousers. Their weapons were clean and their bodies strong. Father said they came from Belgium and Canada – Bangladesh and Ghana too. I took down the atlas from the bookcase and found all those countries on the map. I was amazed that soldiers had come from so far to help Rwanda.

Before Christmas I learnt from reading the newspaper that the President still hadn't signed the peace agreement he'd approved in August. That seemed strange. By the New Year the RPF was threatening to break the ceasefire if the President didn't sign soon, and by February people were rioting again in the streets.

By the time I was fourteen and March had turned into April, the President still hadn't signed. Joseph called the time between August and April "*igihirahiro*", which meant "hesitation" and "uncertainty". Every night he would listen to the Vampire Radio in the yard, then sniff and rub his eyes before turning it off and staring into the star-filled sky.

* * *

On 6th April I was woken, as usual, by the sound of Joseph's boots as he walked down the side of the house and through the garden towards home. He didn't whistle – his silence gave a feeling of eeriness to the damp morning air.

A stillness in my butterfly farm drew my eye to it. And there, crouching beside it, I found, for the second time, my *Charaxes acræoides* dead.

It was then I remembered an entire section in *African Butterflies* about pinning and setting, which I'd read and wanted to try. It felt like the only thing to do. Since we hadn't set it free I would immortalize it instead.

At the dining-room table I laid out all the materials that I had in my collection kit. I placed the spreading board in front of me and held the butterfly by its thorax so as not to damage its wings. Very gently I pierced a pin through it. I put it in the middle of the spreading board and turned the cog to hold it tight. When the groove was the same width as its body, I stopped turning and pushed the pin into the cork base.

It was secure on the board, its wings spread open.

I moved a forewing upwards, then positioned a pin at the top and repeated the process on the opposite side. Once the forewings were in place, I began work on the hindwings. I then moved the antennae into place and pinned those too. Finally, I put two small slips of paper over its wings. The butterfly was now fully prepared. I sat back and admired my work. It was strangely satisfying seeing it laid out in perfect symmetry. All that remained was for me to leave it to dry for twenty-four hours.

But as hard as I tried, I couldn't wait that long, and after dinner I took the small frame from the kit and laid it down, like a coffin, next to the spreading board.

One by one I removed every pin, except the one through its thorax, and carefully transferred the butterfly into the collection frame. I wrote out a small card with its name, place and date of death.

Charaxes acræoides

Rwanda

6th April 1994

I was admiring my butterfly, considering how to show and tell Beni, when a scream from the kitchen made me leave what I was doing and run to see what was happening.

I found Fabrice in the corner of the kitchen, his hands over his mouth, his eyes wide with shock, trembling and staring at the radio.

"What is it, Fabrice?" asked Mother, who had come running too.

Fabrice didn't reply.

"Fabrice?"

"Eh, Madame," he said eventually, in a very quiet voice. "The President is dead."

At eight thirty that evening, the President's plane was shot down above the airport in Kigali. For the rest of the night, we sat in the dim light of the kitchen listening to the radio. With Fabrice's help, Mother was able to understand that the plane had been struck by two missiles. No one on board had survived. We sat so mesmerized by the radio that we failed to notice the passing of time. It was only when Fabrice said he must head back to his family that Mother and I realized Father hadn't returned home.

25

APRIL 1994

The following day nobody came to work. No baskets were made, no bouquets were tied or taken to Kigali by bus. No pans banged in the kitchen, no scritch-scratch of a broom. I missed the sound of Joseph's boot slapping against his calves.

Most of the day, Mother wandered about the house saying: "I can't believe it, I really can't" – and she'd stare out the window for minutes at a time. I assumed she was waiting for Father – but he never came. Father would be safe in Kigali, I reassured myself, staring at my butterfly in its frame with the pin through its chest.

After seeing or hearing nobody all day, I was surprised when Joseph knocked on the back door for his six-o'clock shift.

"Very bad, Madame," he said, when Mother asked him what he knew. Joseph was unable to say more in his broken English, but it was clear by his haunted expression that the news from outside was not good.

He went to his lookout, lit the fire and hunkered down in the rain.

In the morning I woke not to the sound of the cockerel or Joseph's slapping boots, but to a noise I hadn't heard before: a jeering and banging from the road. I opened my curtains a peep to see a crowd of teenage boys at the bottom of the garden, shouting and screaming and shaking their fists. They waved clubs and machetes and held bottles of beer.

I ran to Mother's bedroom. She wasn't there. *Mother, Mother*, I shouted within myself, racing through the house. I found her in the back lobby.

"Stay here, Arthur," she said, doing up her coat. "Lock the door behind me. Do you understand?"

I did as she said and took Romeo to the lounge. We watched from the window.

"What do you want?" yelled Mother at the crowd of boys. Sweat began to seep from my brow. I was terrified that something would happen to her and I'd be left entirely on my own. Where was Joseph when we needed him? Why wasn't he helping Mother?

The boys were looking for someone – accusing Mother of hiding people.

"Joseph! Thomas!" they yelled.

"Joseph and Thomas aren't here," said Mother – and I wondered if that was true. Had Joseph gone early? I hadn't heard him leave.

Losing patience with Mother, the boys pushed past her and charged towards the house. There was nothing she could do. With their clubs they smashed the glass of the front door. I crawled under the dining-room table and huddled in a ball. Boys my age, with whom I should have gone to school, whom I often passed on the road, spread like shrapnel round the house.

"Get out!" screamed Mother. From under the tablecloth I watched her grab them by their faded T-shirts and push them towards the door.

From the bedrooms came the thud of beds being over-turned, wardrobes wrecked, cupboards thrown open and their contents tossed on the floor. I heard Father's desk being tipped up, his papers scattered. From my hiding place I watched the two remaining boys search behind the sofa, pull the shelves from the walls and kick books around the room.

"Eh, Sammy," came a voice, which I recognized immediately.

Zach, with his bloodshot eyes, was staring directly at the table. Sammy stood a step behind.

"*Mzungu…*" he said. It sounded as if he was trying to tease me out. "*Mzungu…*"

I was too big to go unnoticed. I could stay where I was and let them knock the table over or I could crawl out on my hands and knees. I chose the latter and stood up. I was surprised to find myself as tall as Zach, maybe taller.

"Joseph. Thomas," he grunted at me. "*Où?*"

Even if I'd known where they were, I wasn't going to show them. It was then I remembered playing hide-and-seek with Beni. If Joseph and Thomas were on the plantation, then it would be extremely hard to find them in the flower fields. I went to the back of the house, unlocked the door and pointed out back. The two boys took off, Zach's machete held high, howling like jackals, soon followed by the others.

With the house quiet I went to my room. There I found my butterfly farm upside down, the contents scattered about the floor. And the glass of my newly framed butterfly was smashed.

I sat on my bed and took it all in.

When I was ready, I swept up the mess and the broken glass and found, in the corner of my room, my book. It had been tossed aside, its pages crumpled – a handful of them completely torn out.

I knelt down. Smoothed the pages. Closed it and held it tight all morning.

Mother and I spent the afternoon trying to bring the house back to normal and listening anxiously to the radio. I managed to find the English station with the faraway voice, so that Mother could understand too. It was announced that anarchy now reigned in Kigali. There was that word again. I looked it up.

Anarchy /ˈænəkɪ/ n. a situation in which there is no organization and control, especially in society.

I thought only of Father. Was he at work or had he found a safe place to stay? Mother continued to glance at the telephone. It never rang.

We sat by the fire and listened to the news that cabinet ministers had been kidnapped, the Prime Minister killed and ten Belgian peacekeepers murdered. Nuns, journalists, the well-spoken, people who owned cars – anyone who might be Tutsi or a Tutsi sympathizer – were being slaughtered in the streets. We listened and understood, but couldn't imagine the horror.

Hutu extremists were spreading across the country, rounding up young men and filling them with hate towards the Tutsis. The poor and the homeless joined the *interahamwe* – "those who attack together". They were slaughtering Tutsis as freely as animals and holding feasts to celebrate their work.

As the sun set that Friday evening, I realized Romeo wasn't in the house. I went to the back door, clapped my hands and waited: he didn't come. Taking the torch, I headed out to the yard, shining light into every corner. He wasn't there. I opened the gate to the vegetable garden and picked my way over the rutted ground.

The light from my torch revealed the rhubarb, artichoke and cabbage plants, but there was no sign of Romeo. When I reached halfway down the path I heard a disturbance near the cutting shed, but a snuffling sound distracted me. I threw a beam of light over the cabbages and found

Romeo standing in the middle of the patch, gnawing on something. As I got closer, I trod on a rubber boot, strewn aside. I examined it under the light, then shone the torch from side to side. Something beneath me crunched. The torch revealed a hand. And there, cast aside like a loose, green cabbage, was Joseph's head. His eyes were wide, his gappy teeth knocked out, his jaw gaping: it was as if he was frozen in a silent scream. Romeo was lapping an open gash on his neck. I stumbled out of the cabbage patch unable to catch a breath.

* * *

In the morning I was mumbling: words tried to break out of me. I didn't feel the need to fight them – they didn't gag me: they sat silently at the back of my mouth.

The images of the night before came flooding back: the sight of Joseph's face, his flesh; the sound of Romeo lapping up his blood. But still I waited for him to walk through the garden – his boots slapping. A dull, all-consuming ache filled my chest when I realized he'd never come, when I realized I'd never hear that sound again.

In the living room Mother was on the couch, staring into nothing. She was wearing the same clothes as the day before: she hadn't been to bed. She asked me to sit beside her for a while. I didn't mind. I didn't feel like eating my bananas and toast anyway.

"Arthur," she said in a voice almost devoid of life. "I need you to be brave." I thought of my name – which meant courage – and allowed her to hold my hand. "Thomas is dead too."

Mother didn't go into details, but I found out from listening to the few mourners who were able to come that he was found in the cutting shed, his long limbs thrown into buckets like cut flowers. Sitting with Mother on the couch I wished for the humdrum of Saturday chores, of peeling potatoes and scrubbing floors.

Though it felt as though time had stopped, the hours slipped by. The radio said that a new government had been formed, that UN soldiers in their blue helmets were watching people being slaughtered without firing their guns, and that French and Belgian troops had arrived to evacuate their nationals. None of this made sense. I longed for Father to come home and explain it all to me. But he didn't.

Around lunchtime Fabrice arrived.

"Madame," he said. "I need your help."

"Anything," said Mother.

"It is Celeste. She is not safe. You hide her?"

"Of course. Bring her and her family straight away."

"Eh Madame, no safe to walk. Gangs everywhere. They will kill."

"But I can't drive," said Mother, looking at her ankle, which she had twisted badly while chasing the teenage intruders.

Fabrice cast his eyes over me.

"Arthur," Mother said. "Do you think you could drive us there? It's only a short distance, and they wouldn't attack our car."

I knew I could. I ran to the back door and grabbed the keys. Mother limped behind with Fabrice.

In the truck I put down the clutch and turned the key. The engine shattered the silence. I put it into gear, pressed the gas and lifted the clutch just as Mother had taught me to do. Off we went – Fabrice, Mother and me – down the drive and onto the road.

The shops had been abandoned: the doors kicked in and stock looted. The yellow-eyed ladies were not there any more. The bar on the corner was surrounded by men listening to the radio. When we passed, they whooped and jeered and brandished clubs in the air.

The school was empty, its door wide open, the schoolteacher nowhere to be seen; the President's picture hung graffitied on the wall; the map of Rwanda was torn on the ground.

At Fabrice's house there was no sign of Beni. The goats were gone, the neat rows of potatoes pulled up and the machete that once glimmered in the sun was missing.

"What about your family?" asked Mother.

"They are safe, Madame. Do not worry."

I wondered where they were, but trusted Beni was fine.

"*Ici*, Arthur," said Fabrice, just a little way past his house and before the church. "This is it."

"Round the back," said Mother. "Out of sight."

I drove the pickup between Celeste's shack and the neighbouring one into the field behind.

"Keep engine running," said Fabrice, jumping out and going into the house.

Mother bit her fingernails and glanced all around.

"Hurry, hurry," she said to no one, constantly checking the mirrors.

It couldn't have been more than a minute that Fabrice was gone, but it felt like an hour. The relief when he reappeared with Celeste, leaning on her *fimbo*, and her husband and family was immense.

Fabrice pulled out the tarpaulin from the back of the truck and instructed them to lie on the metal floor. One by one they lay down as neat and compact as matchsticks in a box. Fabrice covered them up, then casually sat on top of them as if they were sacks of tea. He banged his fist on the cab of the pickup: his instruction for me to go.

The ruts and potholes I hadn't noticed on the way to Celeste's now seemed the size of craters. I felt every bounce and bump as if I too were lying flat in the back covered in plastic.

As we approached the bar, the crowd of men broke into the road and waved us down.

"Don't stop, Arthur," said Mother. "Keep going. If we stop they'll search the back."

Doing as Mother said I took a deep breath and put my foot down. We charged through the men, kicking up dust and scattering them like skittles.

"Well done!" cried Mother when we were through and clear. I felt a little proud. "Well done, you!" she cheered.

I took the pickup round the back. Before I'd stopped, Fabrice was out and removing the tarpaulin. Celeste's family hauled themselves up and ran towards the house. Celeste hobbled behind as quickly as she could, her flip-flops slapping. Once inside, Mother opened the hatch to the attic and stowed all twelve of them away.

It wasn't long until the crowd of men from the bar caught up with us. They searched the outbuildings and fields, then gathered in the yard. Fabrice went out to talk to them. Mother and I watched from the kitchen.

Fabrice shook his head and pointed in the direction of Celeste's house, causing the men to push him.

"You are Hutu," said their leader, shoving him with the butt of a club. I wanted Fabrice to shove him back. "But you are a Tutsi lover. Show us the Tutsi and her family."

"She has no family," replied Fabrice. "You ask Madame."

The leader of the gang came to the back door with Fabrice. Mother opened it.

"Madame," said Fabrice. "Celeste, she has family?"

Mother shook her head and said to the man, who I realized was the schoolteacher: "Celeste never married" – and shut the door.

We returned to our lookout at the window and watched the men gather in a huddle. After a while the schoolteacher approached Fabrice and said: "Show us this woman, or we kill your family – your Tutsi-loving family."

I wanted Fabrice to show them Celeste and her family so that nothing would happen to Beni. But then I felt terrible when I pictured Celeste lying dead like Joseph or Thomas, with her head chopped off or her limbs in buckets.

"Show us," they said, beating Fabrice with clubs and threatening to send word for his family to be killed. I could hardly watch.

After several blows Fabrice lifted his head and walked to the door. He came in, went to the loft and returned with Celeste. They went out to the yard.

"I prove to you," said Fabrice to the leader, "I am no Tutsi lover."

Fabrice took the schoolteacher's club, raised it up and brought it down on Celeste's back. Crack. Celeste fell to the ground. Thud. Mother screamed. I froze. I watched Fabrice take a *machete* from another man and swing it into Celeste's side as if simply clearing corn.

Celeste lay lifeless, blood seeping into her T-shirt. Colour deserted her face like a butterfly fading from cyanide. I watched her slip away.

"This man has a Tutsi wife," shouted one of the men from the crowd, seeming not to notice Celeste.

I panicked. I knew it was true. Fabrice was married to a Tutsi: Beni's family tree said so.

"Is this true?" asked the schoolteacher.

Fabrice nodded.

The schoolteacher pressed his face right up against Fabrice's and said: "If you are not a Tutsi lover, then you will kill your family too."

Fabrice answered him immediately: "Go to my house. Bring my family here and I will kill them."

I couldn't believe my ears.

The men ran off, jumping over Celeste's body as though she was nothing more than a sack of rice. Fabrice came to the back door, took Mother by the hand and led her to Celeste. I followed. Bending down beside her, Fabrice shook her gently. Celeste released a groan.

"My God," said Mother. "She's alive?"

Fabrice helped her to her feet and said, "Those men see what they want to see."

"You wounded her to save her life?"

"Yes, Madame," he said and took Celeste's weight, helping her into the house.

With Celeste on the sofa, Fabrice asked to talk to Mother in the kitchen. I was left to wrap a sheet tight round Celeste's side and make her comfortable. "Thank you, Arthur," she said, looking at me warmly, managing the faintest gummy grin. "Good boy." I sat beside her and watched her drift into sleep.

Mother returned soon after and said: "Lock all the doors, and don't open them to anyone." She then dashed out the back door with Fabrice.

Half an hour or more passed before Mother and Fabrice returned. They smelt of petrol. Only moments later the schoolteacher and his men arrived back too. They were angry and shouting.

"Your family wasn't there," said the schoolteacher. "You tricked us."

"They came here while you were gone," said Fabrice, and Mother nodded. "Come. See."

I followed Fabrice, Mother and the mob through the gate and out to the pyre that was burning by the cutting shed. It smelt different from usual. It wasn't the woody smell of garden remains: it was acrid. As I got closer I could make out the shape of contorted limbs, stiff like branches, burning to ash.

"There," said Fabrice pointing to the pyre.

"What?" asked the schoolteacher.

With a poker Fabrice pulled out a melting identity card. The schoolteacher took it, read what it said, then tossed it aside.

I took a step closer to the flames to see the card for myself. In the ash and dirt I saw two big almond eyes staring up from the melting, distorted plastic.

Beni was dead.

26

I ran to my bedroom and lay on my bed, numb. It was as if when Beni's spirit left her body, mine did too. How could Mother and Fabrice have done such a thing? It made no sense at all.

"Arthur," Mother called several times that night, knocking gently on my door. I jammed a chair under the handle to prevent her from getting in. I felt as lifeless as an empty seed pod blowing in the wind. Nothing Mother had to say could make me feel any better.

I still felt numb the next morning when the Belgian soldiers arrived, banging on the front door. They insisted Mother and I leave with them immediately.

"*Cinq minutes*," we were told. Five minutes to pack our things.

A soldier with a gun across his chest stood guard at the front door. I didn't understand why soldiers were protecting us but not the Tutsis. Were we more important than them?

"Quickly, Arthur," said Mother, taking down a small suitcase from the attic, where Celeste's family had remained all night. They had eaten only dry bread and water and had not come down once, not even to go to the toilet. They were still up there.

"Get your toothbrush and some soap."

Spurred on by the presence of the soldier, I did as she said and took them to my bedroom, where she packed them with my weekly clothes and passport, nothing more. I took my butterfly, pinned, set and framed, and handed it to her. She looked at it twice, placed it on top of my belongings and zipped up the case.

I stared into my butterfly farm, empty and lifeless.

"Come on, Arthur. There isn't time."

By the farm was my book. I picked it up and went to the front door.

"He's ready," Mother said to the guard.

"*Et vous?*"

"I'm staying."

"*Non, Madame.*" The soldier used the barrel of his gun to direct Mother towards the convoy of military vehicles parked at the bottom of the garden, but she wouldn't budge. She looked into my eyes, placed her hand on my shoulder and said: "Arthur, be brave."

She then ruffled my hair the way Father used to do. I wished he were there with us. All I wanted was to hear his big, booming laugh. Maybe, I thought, Father would be wherever I was going, maybe Father could explain what Fabrice and Mother had done.

"Say goodbye to Romeo, Arthur." The words caught in Mother's throat. I picked him up and nuzzled my cheek against his. He tried to lick my face, but I wouldn't let him – the image of him lapping Joseph's blood was burnt in my memory. Mother gave me a kiss, then wrapped her arms around us and squeezed tight. I wanted to squeeze her back, but couldn't.

"The soldiers will look after you," she said, letting me go.

"Madame," said the soldier. "It's not safe. You are married to a Belgian Tutsi. You and your child are not safe here. You must leave."

The soldier was right. The Vampire Radio had been talking about the "Belgian Bandits", and how it didn't matter if they were killed. "If we kill some of them, the rest will leave," one man had said.

"My decision is final," said Mother.

I wanted to pack Mother's suitcase and make her come with me, but there was nothing I could do. Her mind was made up. A shout of "*Allez*" came from the lead lorry. The soldier stared at her a moment longer, but Mother shook her head.

I was led down the path, away from Mother and Romeo, from home and everything I knew, past the yellow roses and hydrangea bushes, whose flowers had been lopped off by machetes and lay scattered on the ground.

A soldier hauled me into the back of the lorry, which had a wooden frame with a canvas cover, like an elephant's ribcage and hide. There were lots of other white people: I only recognized Dr Sadler, and sat down next to him, clutching my book. As the soldier got in, I caught one last glimpse of Mother. She was standing in front of our ivy-covered bungalow, waving me off, her smile wide, her eyes brimming with tears.

* * *

The convoy moved slowly away from home. We wound our way through local farmers who lined the road, armed with clubs and spears. They shook their fists as we passed, chasing us with hatred in their eyes. The women in the lorry were clinging onto the hands of soldiers and sobbing uncontrollably. I clung to my book.

We passed the shops, the bar, the school. I couldn't bring myself to look at Beni's house for fear my numbness might turn to pain. At the church the doors were open: it was full. Crowds of Tutsis pushed in. The giant cross that once hung slantwise above the altar now lay on the ground. The priest and elders closed the doors, kicking Tutsis away into the hands of machete-wielding Hutus. Men who had sat side by side on pews now raised machetes above their neighbours' heads.

The lorry swept past. I didn't look back.

The road to town looked like a river of people. It was as though the whole population of Rwanda was on the road with their possessions. Women carried bedding, firewood, plastic basins, pot and pans. Men dragged weary-looking livestock, barely clinging to life. Teenagers carried jerrycans and children; children carried babies, babies cried for milk. The people no longer dawdled because they weren't in a hurry: they dawdled because they were weak, almost hollow.

I sat in the lorry with the white people, our belongings neatly packed in cases.

We were passing the fields of blue tents when the lorry stopped. Through the small plastic window that separated the back of the lorry from the cab I could see a large tree trunk across the road. Men in baggy coloured suits and clown wigs waved rifles in the air. I knew from the radio descriptions that they were *interahamwe*. They were not like the men Mother and I had seen a few months before, men who neither could read nor knew what they were looking for: these men were organized, systematic, cold.

I felt sick. The women panicked, their husbands held them close. A stocky man in a red wig, who stank of sweat and beer, swaggered up to the truck. It was Simon.

He scanned our faces one by one and spat on the floor.

"Look," he said in his loud voice, and waved a rifle at a pile of bodies stacked as neatly as Jenga blocks, their clothes soaked with blood. The stench entered my nostrils and never left.

"We kill the cockroaches," he said, and turned his attention to a scuffle behind him. A man, tall and thin, with a long nose like Father's, was explaining that he had lost his identity card.

"Kill him," said Simon.

"*Oya*," he pleaded, sinking to his knees. "I promise, I am Hutu."

"You look like Tutsi scum."

Simon's machete was about to fall when the man yelled: "I give you all my money if you shoot me, please."

He began emptying his pockets of everything he had. Coins jangled to the ground, notes fluttered in the breeze. Simon put his rifle to his head and pulled the trigger. Dead.

The women on the truck screamed, others turned pale. The men mostly looked at the floor. The people walking on the road simply walked past the dead man. They'd seen it all before. Simon and his accomplices slung him onto the pile. It was over quicker than it had begun.

As the truck moved forward, I thought about how it might feel to kill a human. Did it feel the same as killing a butterfly? Was it like the cyanide death – quick and easy, the blood draining, the colour fading and regret creeping in? Or was it more like the chloroform death – a smothering guilt? Was there any satisfaction in an effortless death that looked like sleep – a death that only became real when the rot set in and the stench was thicker than the blue flies on the brown skin of the dead?

I wondered who would tend to the bodies as I had tended to my butterfly.

The lorry moved on, past endless corpses strewn by the road – men, the elderly, pregnant women, children, babies – no one had been spared. Limbs chopped off, heads smashed in, bodies burnt alive.

Dr Sadler uttered reassurances gently by my side.

In town the petrol station stood empty, but no sign swung in the breeze. The windows were smashed and the pumps pulled out. The mango tree in the corner had been stripped of all its fruit. I wondered if Sammy had gone to the border and if his *mama* and *data* had gone too.

We passed Madame Dubois's house: her hedge was overgrown – the words "I Love Jesus" could no longer be read.

At the post office, bodies clogged the storm drain. I wondered if the postmaster was safe, or dead beneath the counter. And at the hotel, Mr Umuhoza was standing at the gates, which people clambered over. As we passed, he opened them and let the people through.

Lake Kivu was brown with waste; bloated bodies were bobbing on its surface.

We slowed as the truck moved through the crowds towards the border. Another roadblock lay ahead. Sebazungu was stopping the traffic like a policeman. He stood with a machete held up to the sky with paper-work in his hand.

"They've got a list of the people they want," said a man to his wife.

Dr Sadler whispered in my ear: "Lie down, Arthur. Under the bench."

I knew not to disobey. Even though I wanted to see what was happening, I got down and slid under the bench, the fabric of ladies' skirts keeping me hidden.

"Albert Baptiste?" called Sebazungu, who jumped into the back of the lorry. His eyes were red as poppies. It was as if the Devil had entered his soul. I thanked God Father wasn't here. If he were he'd have been a dead man. I held my breath and listened to people saying they hadn't seen him.

"Cockroach," he said, and spat his hate out the back of the truck. It landed by a bright-red shoe.

Fabrice!

The crowd was so big it swarmed past the truck, pushing Fabrice forward and out of view. I scanned thousands of frightened faces until I saw him again – and with him was Beni.

Beni wasn't dead!

I rolled out from my hiding position and got up as quickly as I could, desperate for Beni to see me, but Sebazungu caught me by the neck and pressed a machete against my throat.

"Arthur Baptiste," he sneered, shoving me to the back of the truck. His scar – the shape of a new moon – pressed against my cheek.

I didn't hear what he said next. I was too focused on Beni, who waved to me from below. I wanted to wave back, but Sebazungu had my hands locked behind me. The cold metal blade of his machete nudged deep into my skin. I didn't think about dying. I thought only that Beni was by far the prettiest girl in the crowd. She was even more beautiful than our butterfly.

A group of *interahamwe* pointed at Beni. Zach was with them, wearing a barbaric grin. Sammy was there too. They jostled and laughed their way towards her like frenzied hyenas.

"This boy is with me. Let him go," Dr Sadler said to Sebazungu. "He is English."

"He has Tutsi blood."

The *interahamwe* drew closer to Beni. She couldn't see them coming. I stared straight at them in the hope that she would follow my eyes. Words formed at the back of my throat and rolled to the tip of my tongue. This time it wasn't the words that choked me. It was Sebazungu.

"Don't kill that one: she's a perfect little whore," I heard Sammy say.

"Better a dead Tutsi whore than a live one," replied Zach, and the others jeered and whistled.

A surge of emotion pulsed round my body, and I fought with Sebazungu, who pressed the machete deeper into my throat, until I could barely breathe.

"Let him go. Keep me instead," insisted Dr Sadler.

"What use are you?"

"I can treat your men."

Sebazungu thought about this for a moment, then conceded.

He set me free.

At the tailgate I saw Zach raise a machete above Beni's head. Suddenly my teeth came apart, my jaw loosened, a surge of energy rushed up my throat and words burst out of me.

"Run, Beni!" I screamed. "Run to the cave!"

The release of adrenalin from those few words consumed me. Beni ran, as fast as she could, followed by Zach and the others. I was about to jump from the truck to chase after them when Dr Sadler stopped me.

"No!" he shouted and held on to my shirt. "It's not safe for you to stay."

Sebazungu got off and pulled the doctor down. I was left clinging to the frame. The truck jerked forward and started moving off.

I watched Beni being chased by the gang and willed her to run faster.

"Run, Beni," I called. "Run!"

In my panic I didn't notice my book slip from my pocket. Too late to catch it, I saw it fall to the ground, into the mud, and be trampled by the crowd.

"Goodbye, Arthur," called Dr Sadler, waving me off. He grew smaller – Rwanda slipped away.

As it crossed the border the truck was rocked by an almighty boom: Nyiragongo had erupted. The sky grew dark with ash.

It felt very much as though the giant had woken and turned out the light of the world.

Epilogue

Twenty years have passed since I left Rwanda. I was taken into Goma and flown to London, where my uncle and his family met me. They were just as they appeared in their Christmas photos – denim jeans, Mickey Mouse sweatshirts and grimacing smiles. I was immediately sent to boarding school, which was every bit as dreadful as Father made it out to be.

I thought of my parents every day, searching news reports for any scrap of evidence that they were still alive. There was nothing. Only images of men loading rotting bodies into garbage trucks. Rwanda and its people had been torn apart.

And I thought of Beni. With every breath I thought of Beni. I wondered if she had made it to the cave, if she had managed to outrun the gang and find her way to safety. It was impossible to think of anything else.

Three months passed without any communication from Mother: no letters, telegrams or phone calls. It was almost autumn in England when I finally received a letter. The news was both good and bad.

She told me that the postmaster and his family had been killed, even though they were Hutus. He was drowned in the cesspool behind his home for allowing his neighbours to hide in one of his cupboards.

The schoolteacher flushed his Tutsi pupils out of their homes. They were lined up and killed by the *interahamwe* one by one.

Mr Umuhoza was spared, due to his ability to supply drink and accommodate prostitutes for the extremists. As a result he was able to shelter thousands of Tutsis in the hotel. They survived on water from the pool and what goods he was able to bring in from Goma.

The priest, who helped slaughter hundreds with hand grenades in the church, escaped and was rumoured to be living comfortably abroad.

Celeste survived the injuries that Fabrice had inflicted on her to save her life. She and her family remained in Mother's attic for many weeks. A Hutu neighbour risked his own life by sneaking in to provide them with food rations and water – which were increasingly scarce. They were eventually rescued and taken to the refugee camp in Goma.

As for Fabrice and his family – well, that news I read with the greatest interest of all. Mother told me how Fabrice had thought up the idea of dousing the dead on the plantation in petrol and passing them off as his family. They then hid in the cave for three months and wouldn't have survived if it weren't for Sammy, who left provisions for them in the tunnel. He had never intended to hurt Beni that night at the hotel – it was all a ruse. He knew if he was seen as a moderate Hutu he'd be killed.

Sammy was Beni's saviour, and he was not alone. Among all the butchery, savagery and loss of life were a million acts of compassion and bravery. Sammy's kindness and Beni's survival were rays of hope in a country enveloped in gloom.

As the years passed, Mother continued to send letters telling me what news she had. She wrote when Simon was put on trial by the *gacaca* court and imprisoned. He had killed scores at the roadblock and many on the plantation too, including Thomas. Mother said he no longer wore blue dungarees: instead, he could be seen ploughing at the roadside in pink uniform – the colour worn by the genocide prisoners. Zach was imprisoned too for killing Joseph, among others.

Sebazungu avoided prison – even though, or perhaps because he was one of the principal organizers of the massacres in the area. He continues to live near the plantation, side by side with the Tutsi family members of those he ordered to be killed.

Throughout the massacres Dr Sadler remained in the country, one of only thirty whites who did. He kept his promise and treated the killers as well as their victims. Though I didn't realize it at the time, Dr Sadler played a crucial role more than once in my life. It was he who was present at my birth, introduced me to lepidopterology and saved me from certain death that day.

Mother confessed to me years later that Dr Sadler was in love with her. Though she was fond of him, and always tried to keep up appearances, she wouldn't allow herself to dishonour Father, despite his transgressions. She stayed with the doctor during the worst of the troubles, but returned to the plantation after the fighting died down. She waited by the phone for months for any news of Father, but no news ever came. Dr Sadler died five years after the genocide, leaving Mother, once again, alone.

To this day neither Mother nor I know what happened to Father. He was a scientist, working on the earliest research into AIDS, which in the 1980s was already growing out of control in Rwanda. The Hutu extremists were suspicious of intellectuals: they believed they "thought too much" and were therefore prone to liberal views. Even if Father had managed to escape Sebazungu that day at the border, we can only assume that, as a known half-Tutsi, he was one of the million victims of the war. I still cling to the hope that he managed to escape and might now be living in exile with a new family.

But of course the news I relished most was that of Beni. Whenever a letter arrived I'd skim-read it to see if there was any mention of her name. All too often there was not. And then one day, many years ago, a letter came telling me that Beni had married a Hutu – one with lots of cows! I didn't know how I felt. All I could think of was something Mother once said: "Catching them's the easy part: it's releasing them that's hard. You never know which way they're going to fly."

The flower plantation, much like Rwanda, slowly began to blossom. With half the population gone, Mother found it difficult to recruit new staff – and those she did had to be trained from scratch. Thanks to her determination it is now a flourishing business again, in which Hutus and Tutsis work side by side.

As for me, I chose to dedicate my life to butterflies, working as a lepidopterist. Though I found my voice that day at the border, I never grew socially confident. I exist between work and home, where I sit most nights alone in my study, staring at the most perfect find of my life:

Charaxes acræoides
Rwanda
6th April 1994

African Butterflies is now as treasured as the butterfly – my memory of Beni, complete.

Acknowledgements

I wish to thank:

Louisa and Reuben Culpin for introducing me to Rwanda, everyone at the Imababazi Orphanage for their kindness and hospitality, and those in Gisenyi who welcomed me.

My husband Peter for giving me the time and freedom to write this book and for understanding when either I or my mind was far from home.

Simon Kerr and the Lightship judges: Alessandro Gallenzi, Simon Trewin and Tibor Fischer for seeing the potential in my work and for their guidance, straight-talking encouragement and support.

My tutors at Bath Spa: Richard Kerridge, Andrew Miller and Tricia Wastvedt for noticing the things I didn't.

Those far more qualified to write about Rwanda than me: Dallaire, Gourevitch, Keane, Carr and Prunier, all of whose work informed my own.

The dedicated, meticulous and hard-working team at Alma, but in particular Alessandro, who steered me with a gentle hand through the editing process.

My Mum and Dad for looking after our newborn son so that I might stare bleary-eyed at my computer.

And finally, Rwanda – a place forever in my heart.